Th … iles™

More Armada two-in-ones from HarperCollins

The Nancy Drew Files

Hit-and-Run Holiday
White Water Terror

Deadly Doubles
Two Points to Murder

False Moves
Buried Secrets

Heart of Danger
Fatal Ransom

Trial by Fire
Never Say Die

Carolyn Keene

The Nancy Drew Files™

Stay Tuned for Danger

Circle of Evil

Armada
An Imprint of HarperCollins*Publishers*

Stay Tuned for Danger and *Circle of Evil*
were first published in the USA by
Simon & Schuster Inc. in 1987
First published in Great Britain in Armada 1991
First published together in this edition in 1995
by HarperCollins Children's Books
1 3 5 7 9 10 8 6 4 2

HarperCollins Children's Books
is a division of HarperCollins Publishers Ltd,
77-85 Fulham Palace Road,
Hammersmith, London W6 8JB

Acknowledgement is made to Mildred Wirt Benson,
who, writing under the pen name Carolyn Keene,
wrote the original *Nancy Drew* books.

ISBN 0 00 694530 9

Printed and bound in Great Britain by
HarperCollins Manufacturing, Glasgow

THE NANCY DREW FILES™

Case 17

Stay Tuned for Danger

Carolyn Keene

Chapter One

NANCY, YOU'RE DRIVING me nuts! Would you please finish that sundae? Our plane leaves in an hour!" Bess Marvin looked longingly at her friend's dessert. Then she pulled a pink beret over her straw blond hair and reached for the matching pink jacket that was hanging on the back of her chair.

Nancy Drew looked at Bess, her blue eyes sparkling with amusement. "Take it easy, Bess. We're five minutes from the airport. George'll get us there in plenty of time."

Nancy and Bess were flying to New York City to visit Nancy's aunt, Eloise Drew, and

George was dropping them off. It was early, so they had decided to stop for ice cream near the airport.

"Admit it, Bess," George Fayne said with a laugh, throwing an arm around her cousin's shoulders. "You're just jealous because Nancy's eating that fantastic, splendiferous, mouth-watering—"

"Mmmm. And it's so-o-o good," Nancy said, licking her lips.

"Quit teasing, you guys," Bess muttered. "I swear I gain weight just looking at something that fattening."

"It does look good," George said, wistfully agreeing. She and Bess were cousins as well as best friends, but they couldn't have been more different. With her tall, athletic figure, her dark hair and eyes, and her levelheaded approach to life, George was her cousin's opposite in every way.

"When you two get back from New York, we've got to come here again," George said. "You can fill me in on your trip, and by then I'll be able to order something disgustingly rich and gooey. Just like those banana splits we had at that wonderful restaurant, Rumpelmayer's." George sighed. "I wish I were going with you."

"I'll never understand you," said Bess. "How can you pass up a chance to go to New York, the most glamorous city in the world, just so you can run in some stupid race? What's the big deal?"

"Don't be dumb, Bess. I've been training for this race for months. It may only be the River Heights marathon, but it's important to me."

"Yummm," Nancy savored one last mouthful of ice cream before putting down her spoon. "Okay, I'm ready," she said with a toss of her reddish gold hair.

Bess eyed the remains of Nancy's sundae hungrily. "No," she told herself, "I refuse to blow my diet before we even get to New York. I mean, you never know who I might meet," she said, looking at her friends. "In New York, anything's possible."

Nancy and George exchanged knowing smiles. Bess was sure to find cute guys in the Big Apple, just as she did in River Heights.

"Well, if I know Nancy," George said, "you two will probably wind up in the middle of an adventure. Remember the last time we were in New York? We didn't even have time to go shopping!"

George was right. Intrigue and mystery seemed to find Nancy wherever she went. At eighteen, she was already a rising star in the world of detectives.

"No way," Nancy protested. "This time I'm just going to be a tourist. I'm going to spend some time with my aunt, Eloise, do some shopping, see a Broadway show—"

"*A* Broadway show? Are you kidding? There are at least six that I'm dying to see!" Bess exclaimed.

"Hey, you two," Nancy declared, looking at her watch. "Now we had better hurry."

And with that, the three girls paid their bill and filed out of the ice cream shop.

"Here we are," Bess said, staring up at the elegant old apartment building. "This street always looks like a movie set of 'old New York' to me. Like it's a hundred years old, at least."

It was true, Nancy thought. The street had old-world charm, from the tall gingko trees with their fanlike leaves to the old-fashioned gas lamps along the sidewalk that fronted the many brownstone buildings.

"Did I tell you my aunt bought her apartment last year when— Oh, look, there she is!" Nancy cried, waving to her aunt, who was coming out the front door. Tall and elegant, Eloise Drew was a female version of Nancy's father, Carson. They had the same lustrous brown hair and aristocratic features.

"Nancy!" Eloise cried, hugging her niece warmly and planting a kiss on her cheek. "I'm so happy to see you! And Bess," she said, taking Nancy's friend warmly by the hand. "How good it is to see you again. How was your trip?" Eloise asked as they entered the building.

"Kind of boring," Bess admitted with a smile.

"Wonderfully uneventful is more like it," Nancy said in the elevator up to Eloise's second-floor apartment. "I've been so busy lately that it was great just to sit down and leaf through a magazine."

"Well, here we are!" Eloise said, pushing open the door to her apartment. "I've redecorated a bit since you were here the last time."

The apartment was spacious and homey. Bright sunlight splashed across the walls, which were papered in a dainty flowery print.

"I love what you've done!" Bess exclaimed enthusiastically as they were passing through the living room. She paused to look out the window. "I had forgotten there were trees in the backyard!"

"In New York we call it a courtyard. Unfortunately, though, as you probably remember, your room faces the street." Nancy's aunt led them across a small hallway to a cozy bedroom. "Don't worry, the street is usually pretty quiet."

Just then a fire engine came careening down the block, its siren blasting. Eloise waited for it to pass before adding, "Quiet for the city, that is."

The room was all ready for the two girls. Both beds were freshly made with light blue comforters, and two sets of fluffy white towels were neatly folded on top of the modern oak bureau. Eloise slid open a pair of white louvered doors, revealing a nearly empty closet.

"Here you are, ladies," she announced. "And after you've unpacked, we'll have a snack. For dinner, I thought we could go to my favorite Chinese restaurant."

"Super," Nancy said, looking over at Bess, who seemed enthusiastic. "As long as there's no mystery involved, I'm game for anything."

"Well—" Nancy's aunt said hesitantly. "I wouldn't go so far as to say 'no mystery,' Nancy. I was going to save it for later, but since you brought it up . . ."

"Oh, no! I don't want to hear another word. I'm here for a week's vacation, and that's that!" Nancy flung herself on the bed and covered her head with a pillow.

"Okay, okay." Eloise shrugged. "I only thought you'd be interested because it has to do with a TV show. . . ." She stared absently at the ceiling, showing no emotion.

"What TV show?" Bess asked. Nancy's aunt didn't answer. "Come on, Nancy, ask her. I've got to know!"

Nancy peeked out from under her pillow, looking back and forth from Bess to Eloise. "Okay, Aunt Eloise," she muttered. "I give in. What show?"

"Well, let me start at the beginning," the older woman replied, sitting down next to

Nancy. "Yesterday, I happened to tell my downstairs neighbor you were coming to stay with me. Her name is Mattie Jensen, and she's an—"

"*The* Mattie Jensen? Of 'Danner's Dream'?"

Eloise nodded, and Bess nearly fainted with excitement.

"I don't believe it! Mattie Jensen is your neighbor! Is she as beautiful in real life as she is on TV? Is she anything like Serena Livingstone?"

"Hey, wait." Nancy propped herself up on one elbow, looking bewildered. "You guys are way ahead of me! Who's Serena Livingstone?"

Bess looked at Nancy as if she had just arrived from Mars. "That's Mattie Jensen's character on 'Danner's Dream.' Gosh, Nancy, you're really out of it. You at least know who Rory Danner is, don't you?"

Nancy shook her head.

"His real name is Rick Arlen. He and Mattie are the stars of the show," Eloise explained. "Anyway, I told her that you're a detective, and she got very excited."

"Well, is she?" Bess persisted. Nancy and Eloise looked at her, puzzled. "As beautiful in real life, I mean. And as together as Serena?"

"Oh!" Eloise laughed. "Well, let's see. If anything, I'd say she's more beautiful in person. As for together—well, Mattie's a sweet girl, but she's very emotional. I guess you could say she has an artistic temperament."

Eloise turned back to her niece. "Anyway, she was really hoping you would stop by the set. It seems some strange things have been happening to Rick Arlen. She said she could get both of you guest passes for tomorrow morning. If you're willing, that is."

"*If* we're willing? Of course we are!" Bess declared. "I can't believe I'm going to visit the set of 'Danner's Dream'! Wait till George hears about this! She's as crazy about Rick Arlen as I am."

"Don't tell me George watches 'Danner's Dream,' too," Nancy cried in surprise. George was always either training for some athletic event or lost in the pages of a book. How could she have time to watch daytime TV?

"Her mother tapes it for her," Bess explained. "Everybody watches Serena and Rory. They're the hottest couple on the soaps!"

"I think I have heard of them, actually. He was featured in *Chatter* magazine last month, right?" Nancy asked.

Bess nodded. "Blond hair, dazzling blue eyes, muscles out to here," she said, indicating large biceps. "Need I say more?"

"I get the picture," Nancy replied. "But I promised myself—*no mysteries.*"

"Oh, come on, Nancy. How many chances do you get to meet real stars?"

"Well, it would be kind of interesting to see how a television show is put together—"

"Interesting?" Bess cried. "It'll be fantastic! I'll die if we don't go!"

"Then I guess I *can't* say no, can I?" She turned to her aunt. "Okay, you can tell your neighbor we're on."

"Great," said Eloise. "Mattie said you could show up at the studio around ten."

"All right!" Bess exclaimed, her light blue eyes dancing. "Now, I've just got to decide what to wear tomorrow."

"I'd rather check out that snack you were talking about, Aunt Eloise."

"Wait a minute!" cried Bess. "I'm coming, I'm coming. I'll pick out my clothes later."

Nancy had to laugh. Bess was so excited. She just hoped that Mattie Jensen was as prone to exaggeration as Aunt Eloise had said she was. If so, how much of a mystery could there really be?

"Are you sure this skirt fits?" Bess asked. She and Nancy had just walked through the huge glass doors of Worldwide Broadcasting.

"You look fabulous," Nancy assured her friend. All morning Bess had been fussing in front of the mirror, getting ready for their visit to the set of "Danner's Dream." And the results were definitely worth the work. In her soft suede skirt, tights, and ankle boots, Bess looked like a star herself.

"Okay, people," a voice behind them shouted. "We go in here! Make sure your guest pass is visible."

Nancy turned and saw a group of about thirty people push through the same glass doors she and Bess had just entered.

"It's okay, Harry," the tour guide in a navy blue uniform called to the security guard. "They're with me."

"Where you going? 'Danner's Dream'?" the guard asked.

"You guessed it," replied the tour guide.

"It's going to be a zoo in there today," the guard muttered. "But whatever— Management must know what they're doing. Take them into studio one, Joe."

"Well, if I were Serena, I'd kill him," Nancy heard a woman in the tour group say. "I mean, who does that Rory Danner think he is?"

"They may *have* to kill him," her companion replied. "I heard he's leaving the show at the end of the season."

"No!"

"Yes! Didn't you read the *Star Sentinel* last week? He wants to break his contract to make a movie."

"Well, if you ask me, Rick Arlen has gotten

too big for his britches," the first woman said. "We fans count, you know."

At the rear of the group was a large man in an old sweatshirt. He was shifting from foot to foot and muttering, "You'll find out, Rory. You're not that great."

At last they all disappeared through a set of swinging doors. "Boy, they sure seem angry," Nancy remarked.

"That's nothing," the security guard said. "Ever since Arlen decided he was leaving the show, seems like everybody hates him. I wouldn't want to be him right now, no siree." He shook his head. "Can I help you girls?" he finally asked.

"We're here to see Mattie Jensen," Nancy said politely. "She's expecting us."

The guard checked his book. "Miss Drew and Miss Marvin?" he asked. "Let's see—ten o'clock . . . she's probably just going into makeup. It's down the hall and around to your right. First left after the producer's office."

Thanking him, the girls made their way through the set of swinging doors that led into a long hallway. The noisy tour group had gone directly onto the set, but Nancy and Bess continued on, looking for the makeup room.

"This must be the hall he means," said Nancy.

"Maybe we'll pass the casting director's office," Bess whispered, following her.

Just then, two young secretaries stepped into the hall ahead of them. "Well, I think he has a good point!" one was saying to the other.

"He may have a point, but that's still no way to talk to people. Even if he is the producer!"

Feelings seem to be running high everywhere, Nancy thought. Suddenly she grabbed Bess by the wrist and signaled for her to be quiet.

They stopped by an open door with a sign that read William Pappas, Producer. They couldn't see in or be seen. Inside, a man was shouting, probably into a phone since no one responded to him. "I've told you before, he can't do this to me! I don't care if he *is* Rick Arlen. If he leaves this show, he'll never work again! Nobody—*nobody*—breaks a contract with me. I'll kill him before I let him work for someone else!"

Chapter Two

"I can't believe he feels that strongly about Rick Arlen," Bess whispered angrily.

Nancy peered into the office, taking care to remain hidden. William Pappas's face was flushed with anger as he stared at the phone he had just slammed down. He fumbled in his pocket for a cigar.

"Actors! They're all alike! No class—none at all," he muttered to himself. Then he rose and shouted to a timid-looking girl in an inner adjacent office. "Get the writers on the phone and tell them I want a Rory Danner death scene—the more realistic the better. That idiot doesn't deserve to live after what he's put me through! And where's my Danish? You know I can't think before I've had my second coffee."

"Come on!" Nancy said in Bess's ear. "Let's get out of here." They hurried down the long hallway without looking back.

"Gosh, Nancy," Bess announced after they'd rounded a corner and were safely out of sight, "I'll bet he's the one who's causing all the trouble."

"I don't know, Bess. Maybe he has an artistic temperament, too. Remember what my aunt said about Mattie Jensen?"

Bess's attention, however, was caught by something else. "'Makeup.' Here we are." Bess placed her hand over her heart. "I can't believe I'm about to walk through that door and meet Mattie Jensen! How do I look? Are you sure this skirt is okay?"

Nancy couldn't help laughing. "You're too much," she said teasingly. "It *still* looks great, but if you're so uncomfortable why did you wear it?"

"Because it looks great—you just said so yourself!" Taking a deep breath, Bess knocked on the door.

"Come in," someone called out. Bess immediately recognized the voice of her favorite soap opera character.

Inside, Mattie Jensen was sitting in a large, barber-style chair. Her famous auburn curls were wrapped in purple curlers, and her porcelain skin was scrubbed clean. Not a hint of makeup anywhere. But she still looked incredibly beautiful, and her green eyes sparkled.

"Mattie J-Jensen," Bess sputtered.

"You must be Nancy Drew," Mattie replied. She held out a manicured hand and gave Bess a warm smile.

"No, I'm Bess Marvin. She's Nancy."

"Oh, of course," Mattie corrected herself, taking Nancy's hand. "It's great to meet both of you."

"Thanks, same here," Nancy answered.

"Nancy, Bess, I'd like you to meet Kay Wills. She's our makeup artist and one of the great ones. Without her, I'd be lost."

"Come on, Mattie, don't be so modest." Kay rolled her eyes at the girls and began dotting ivory base on Mattie's forehead. "With looks like yours, you'll never be lost."

"Well, looks aren't everything, are they?" Mattie sighed, holding her head still as Kay blended in the foundation.

"Try telling that to your leading man," Kay sniffed, continuing to work.

"Poor Rick," Mattie murmured. "He's so misunderstood. And now all this awful stuff is happening to him. Nancy, maybe you'll be able to help."

Nancy leaned against the wall. "To be honest, Ms. Jensen, I'm in New York on vacation.

I really don't want to get involved in anything complicated."

"Please, call me Mattie. And you've got to help him, Nancy! It's a matter of life and death!"

"You know, you're a lot more upset than he is, Mattie," Kay put in. "As far as I can tell, he loves the attention, no matter how negative it is."

Nancy was puzzled. "If you tell me what's going on, maybe I could give you a few suggestions," she offered. After all, she told herself, giving advice was different from actually getting involved.

"Didn't Eloise tell you?" Mattie asked frantically, her luminous eyes filling with tears. "Someone is trying to kill Rick!"

"Don't cry," Kay ordered, dabbing Mattie's eyes with a tissue. "You'll ruin your makeup."

"Sorry. It's just so upsetting."

"Maybe you should start at the beginning," Nancy said, taking an empty chair next to Mattie.

"It began with the chocolate," Mattie explained, leaning forward. Kay chased after her face with a powder puff. "A box of it came in with the rest of the fan mail one day. Rick is a maniac for chocolate, so he opened the box and ate one right away. It was so bitter that for a minute he thought he'd been poisoned. After a while, though, when he didn't keel over, he figured it was just a practical joke. We all did. But then a letter arrived. It said something like, 'Scared you, didn't I? Good, because this was just a dress rehearsal.' About two days later, a watch came in the mail. It was set at five to midnight, and there was a note attached that said, 'Your time's running out.' You see? Somebody is trying to kill him!"

Mattie was practically standing up in her chair. Kay gently pushed her back down and began working on her eyes. "Take it easy, hon," she said matter-of-factly.

"Maybe this is a stupid question," Nancy ventured, "but has anybody called the police?"

Kay laughed. "If we called the police every time we got a nasty letter around here, we'd be calling them every day! You should see some of the fan mail."

Mattie wheeled around in her chair. "But this is different! These aren't just nasty letters, they're real threats! The trouble is, nobody is taking them seriously!"

"Not even Rick?" Nancy asked.

"Especially not Rick," Mattie said huffily. "He thinks nothing will ever hurt him. As far as he's concerned, the whole thing is the work of a single loony fan out for kicks. I'm the only one who's really worried, and that's why I need your help."

"She'll help you, won't you, Nancy?" Bess

said, not really asking the question. "We'll stay here as long as it takes!"

Nancy smiled wryly. Bess would have promised anything if it meant she could spend more time with her idols.

"But, Bess," she said, protesting. "We have a lot of sightseeing planned, and—"

Just then, the door flew open and Rick Arlen burst in. Bess gasped. He really was even more gorgeous in person. A lock of blond hair had fallen over his forehead, and he impatiently brushed it away. He was holding up a black-and-white glossy photograph of himself. The photo had been scratched almost beyond recognition.

"Mattie," he said, thrusting the picture into her hands, "it's happened again! Look at this!"

Mattie looked at the photo, and at the message scrawled beneath it. " 'If you won't be mine, you won't be anybody's,' " she read. She looked up at Nancy. "You see what I mean?"

"At least it's an old picture," Rick said, trying to make a joke. "It's not even very good, actually."

Bess was standing, absolutely frozen, staring moronically at Rick. Noticing her obvious interest, Mattie hastily introduced the girls to Rick, but it was clear that his mind was on other things. He hardly noticed them.

"Whoever did this has some nerve," he was

saying. "Imagine, tearing up my face like that."

"Please, Rick," Mattie begged, "if you won't call the police, will you at least tell security about this?"

"Come on, now," he said, waving away her concern. "What are they going to do about it? Shake their heads and wring their hands, that's what. Anyhow, it's probably just old man Pappas trying to scare me."

"Rick!" Mattie gasped. "You don't really think—"

"I don't know what to think," he muttered with a shrug. "All I know is that we're scheduled to be on the set in five minutes for dress rehearsal, and I haven't got time for nonsense like this." Rick turned toward the door. Jaw set, eyes ablaze, he was the picture of that perfect romantic rebel, Rory Danner. "See you on the set, Mattie. Oh, and nice meeting you, girls."

He gave Bess and Nancy a cursory nod as he left the room. "What a hunk!" Bess whispered hoarsely. "Oh, Nancy, you've just got to take this case! Just think what might happen to Rick if you don't."

"Bess, sick as it might be, sending hate mail is not a felony."

"Please," Mattie said, breaking in. "Something's very wrong here, I'm sure of it. I'd feel so much better if you'd at least stay and watch this morning's dress rehearsal."

Nancy looked from Mattie to Bess and back again. There was no way they would let her say no. Besides, she reasoned, watching a soap rehearsal was kind of like sightseeing, wasn't it? "Okay, we'll stay," she agreed.

"Oh, Nancy!" Mattie cried happily. "You won't regret this! I promise!"

Nancy hoped not. But she couldn't get rid of the depressing feeling that for the hundredth time, a relaxing vacation was about to be ruined.

On their way to the set, Nancy filled Mattie in on what she and Bess had overheard outside Pappas's office.

"Those two are really on the outs these days," Mattie said. "Ever since Rick got that film deal and gave his notice, it's as though a war has been declared between them. I can't really blame Mr. Pappas, though. The show's ratings depend on Rick. If he goes, 'Danner's Dream' could be in big trouble, and that means trouble for all of us."

"Hmmm." Nancy thought for a moment. "So it's not just Mr. Pappas who's down on Rick."

"Oh, no. In fact, lately it's been Rick against the world." She stopped. "Well, here we are."

Mattie pushed against a vacuum-sealed door. With a *whoosh,* it opened, and the three of them walked onto the set.

Nancy and Bess gazed around the massive studio. In straight rows, rooms that had three walls but no ceilings were set up. Rows of klieg lights hung on suspended bars. Above the lights was a narrow catwalk, and above that, total darkness.

On the ground level, the activity was incredible. Hundreds of cables wound across the floor, and several huge cameras were mounted on dollies. Each one was surrounded by people. On the set of the Danner living room, where the first scene was about to be shot, set dressers were putting the final touches on the scenery. And in the middle of it all stood Rick Arlen. Kay was fussing over his makeup, and he was going over his lines with a script girl. But in case he or anyone forgot a line, a teleprompter stood in either corner of the room. All an actor had to do was cast a glance at one of them and read his lines from the screen.

Nancy and Bess were struck by the strangeness and complexity of it all. They looked dazed as Mattie motioned them to a spot on the floor where they could watch the rehearsal and still be out of the way. Then she disappeared behind the walls of a set.

"Can you believe this?" Bess whispered excitedly.

"Could somebody tell Rick to get on the set, please?" A beautiful black-haired woman barked impatiently into a small megaphone.

"I'm right here, Lillian, dear," Rick purred sarcastically. "What would you like?"

"I hope you bothered to memorize your lines," she snapped.

"Yes, love, I did," he cooed.

"That's what you always say," she said, trying too hard to keep the anger out of her voice. "You shouldn't need a teleprompter, Rick. You're a big boy and a professional."

"If you're referring to that one small incident, Lillian, you'll also recall that I received a death threat that morning. It wasn't exactly my best day."

Suddenly a voice boomed over the set's sound system. "Lillian, back off, will you?"

"Who's that?" Nancy wondered out loud.

A bearded stagehand who was walking by with a line of cables answered her. "That's Luther Parks, the director. He's up there." The stagehand pointed to a Plexiglas booth above the door at the back of the room. "He watches the rehearsal on a bank of TVs up there, and then chooses which camera shots they'll use."

"And who's Lillian?" Nancy asked.

"Ready to roll, ladies and gentlemen," the

director's voice interrupted them. "Let's have quiet on the set, please."

"Places, everyone!" the stage manager yelled. "Charlie, are we locked up?" The man at the door nodded. A bright red light went on above him.

"That light means we're shooting," the same stagehand explained in a soft whisper. With a quick smile, he was gone.

In the silence of the huge studio, Nancy could feel the crackling of tension. For a split second no one moved. Then Rick appeared on the set and sat down on the beige sofa in the Danner living room. With his head in his hands and his elbows on his knees, he looked just like the tortured Rory Danner, brooding over his life. Then Mattie, playing the cool and dignified Serena, appeared in the living room doorway.

"Rory?" she called out softly. "May I come in?"

Rick looked up, but then dropped his head back into his hands. "I don't want to see you, Serena," he growled. "Just get out and leave me alone!"

Mattie stood by the door, cold as ice. "Rory, I have to talk to you—right now." The cameras rolled in for a closeup.

Just then, Nancy noticed a faint shadow moving back and forth on the back wall of the set. She glanced up to see what was causing it. High overhead, she saw a klieg light wobbling wildly on its track. Horrified, Nancy watched as it broke off the bar with a sickening snap and hurtled downward. It was heading right for Rick!

Chapter Three

NANCY STOOD UP and dove across the set, landing on top of Rick. The sofa beneath them toppled over backward. Everyone watched in frozen terror as the heavy lamp hit the floor where the couch had been, shattering into a thousand pieces.

Moments later pandemonium broke out as the cast and crew gathered around the scene of the disaster. Mattie rushed up to Nancy and Rick, who were still in a heap on the floor, gasping for breath.

"Rick! You could've been killed!" Mattie cried. The stage manager was calling for everyone to remain calm on the set, and Bess tried to push her way through a group of stagehands. She stretched, looking to see if Nancy and Rick were okay.

"What in the world is going on around here?" William Pappas hurried onto the set, pushing people aside as he went. "This is all I need! Our insurance rates are high enough as it is!" he muttered angrily. "Is anybody hurt?"

"Nope," Rick replied from his position on the floor. "I was just rescued by this beautiful creature." He looked up at Nancy with a grateful smile. "Hello, gorgeous. Where have you been all my life?"

Nancy turned red to the roots of her hair as she scrambled off Rick and onto her feet. Brushing herself off, she started to push her way through the crowd of onlookers. She had to find Bess.

"Wait!" Rick called after her. "Don't leave me now!" With that, a group of stagehands who were standing nearby broke out in nervous laughter.

Just then Nancy felt a hand on her shoulder. It was Mattie. "Thank heavens you were here. If you hadn't gotten to Rick so quickly . . ." She shivered. Turning to the crowd, she called out, "Everyone, I'd like you to meet Nancy Drew. She's my guest today." Everyone clapped, and Mattie smiled weakly. "And now

I'm going to call security. Maybe they'll believe that someone really is after Rick!" And with a toss of her pretty head, she stepped off the set, headed for the intercom behind the scenery.

"Well, dear, that's one way to meet a star," Lillian observed caustically, glaring at Nancy.

"Wait just a minute—" Nancy began. But then she decided it would be better not to say anything. Lillian might not be the friendliest person she'd ever met, but the last thing Nancy wanted was to make an enemy at the beginning.

Beginning of what? Nancy asked herself. An investigation? Was there really anything to investigate? After all, she reasoned, accidents do happen.

Dodging Lillian's pointed remark, Nancy excused herself and made her way over to the corner of the set. Rick was there, chatting with Bess.

"Ah, my savior!" he said when he saw Nancy. But her quick frown made it clear that she wasn't going to fall for his lines.

"Hey, girls," Rick suggested, "why don't the three of us go back to my dressing room? We can have a soda and get to know each other a little better while they're cleaning up this mess."

"Oh, we'd *love* to!" crooned Bess. Elbowing

Nancy in the ribs, she prompted her friend. "Wouldn't we?"

"I guess that would be all right," Nancy shrugged. Until security had finished looking around, no one would be allowed near the scene of the accident anyway. And maybe she could use the time to find out a little more about Rick Arlen.

"By the way, who was that woman—Lillian somebody—who was so angry at you earlier?" Nancy asked him as they headed down the empty corridor.

"Her name is Lillian Weiss," he hissed, making the name sound snakelike. "She's the assistant director. While Luther is up in the booth playing God, she's his watchdog."

"Sounds like she's not your favorite person."

"She's not. But then, Lillian's just a nobody around here. I don't let her get to me—she's not worth even thinking about."

Just then they came to a door with a polished brass star on it and Rick's name above the star. "Come into my parlor, said the spider to the fly," he quipped lightly. He ushered them in and closed the door quietly behind them.

The bright lights in the dressing room blinded Nancy for a moment when she stepped in.

"I love this room—it's so warm and bright. This is the place I go to get away from the craziness out there." He pointed toward the door. "Let's see, now," he mumbled. "I'd offer you a chocolate, but I'm afraid they're a little bitter. But can I get you something to drink?" Rick opened a small refrigerator.

Bess pushed a lock of blond hair behind her ear before she said, "Okay. Um, a diet soda for me."

"Pour vous?" he asked, turning to Nancy.

"The same, thanks."

"You're a very smart girl. And brave, too. Would you care to marry me?" Rick had taken Nancy's hand gently in his own, and now he offered her a bouquet of imaginary flowers with the other.

Nancy pulled her hand away and looked at him. "I have a boyfriend. Sorry," she said, apologizing.

"Ah—I'm crushed. Well, then," he purred, instantly turning to Bess and taking her hand. "How about you? Would you marry me?"

Bess's eyes twinkled mischievously. "Okay, you're on."

"Oh, you only like me for my looks," Rick complained. Nancy saw him catch a quick glimpse of himself in the mirror before he gazed back at Bess appreciatively. "But then, you're not too bad yourself."

Bess blushed. She seemed to melt into the dressing table as Rick stared at her.

Rick Arlen obviously knew how to flirt, Nancy observed. And Bess was definitely being taken in.

"Well," said Nancy, trying to break the spell, "for a guy who just barely escaped a terrible accident, you're in an incredibly good mood."

"Of course! Of course I am!" Rick said agreeably as he poured the sodas. "I was lucky. That's the best way to be if you're going to be in an accident. Don't you agree? But then, I've always been a lucky guy. I mean, I just met you two, didn't I?"

"Some people don't think the things that have been happening to you lately are accidents," Nancy said.

Rick sank into a plush chair and looked at her impatiently. "Some people are also frightened of their own shadows. Look, when you're a TV star, you have to expect a little craziness. It comes with the territory. Along with a lot of good things, too. Has anyone ever told you that you're beautiful," he added offhandedly to Bess. She almost swooned into his costume rack.

She's really eating this up, Nancy thought. Bess actually seemed to take Rick's baloney seriously.

"Look, I'd better get back to the set," Nancy said, putting down her soda. "Security should have had a good look around by now, and I want to find out exactly what happened. Are you coming, Bess?" she asked.

"Is it okay if I meet you back there in a little while?" Bess responded.

"Don't worry about Bess here," Rick put in with a grin. "I'll take care of her."

That was just what Nancy was afraid of.

Pushing through the thick, soundproof door, Nancy stepped back onto the set. Immediately she saw Mattie trying to break up a fight. One of the men was William Pappas. Nancy hadn't seen the other man before. He was slim, handsome, and at that moment his eyes were ablaze with anger.

"It was an accident!" Pappas was shouting. "Technicians are only human. Now, if you'll get off my back, I'll find out who was responsible and deal with that person. I can't do anything if you're going to stand here and scream at me all day!"

"You *still* don't get it, do you?" the other man shouted back. "Mattie could have been *killed* in there! And I promise you, if so much as a hair on my client's head is ever hurt, your network will be facing the biggest lawsuit the world has ever seen! Come on, Mattie!" He grabbed Mattie's arm and marched toward the door. Nancy ducked behind a piece of scenery and continued to watch.

"Dwayne, please, calm down!" Mattie protested. "No one was trying to hurt me! I was nowhere near the accident!"

"It's the network's responsibility to protect you from things like this, Mattie. Look at those shards of glass! What if one of them had cut your face? Your career would be ruined."

"Nobody is going to get hurt, Dwayne," Pappas said, calmer now. "This is never going to happen again. Now, will you please get out of here so we can clean up this mess and get on with the show?"

As Dwayne stalked off, Nancy heard Pappas remark to Mattie, "It's just my luck that that idiot agent was here today. The last thing I need is a nervous Nellie on the set the day the roof falls in. No offense, Mattie, but the man is a complete fool. Excuse me, please, will you?"

As Pappas breezed by her, Nancy grabbed Mattie's elbow, and they followed him. The producer walked immediately over to the chief of security and began asking questions. Nancy and Mattie got as close as they could without being noticed and listened intently.

"It looks like an accident, plain and simple, Mr. Pappas," the security man was saying.

"Thank you," Pappas muttered. Then he strode directly over to where the lighting technicians were gathered. "Which one of you was responsible for checking the lights this week?" he asked.

"I was," admitted one of the men unhappily. It was the man with the beard who had talked to Nancy and Bess earlier. "But they checked out fine. In fact, just this morning—"

"What's your name?" asked Pappas darkly.

"Uh, MacPherson, Mr. Pappas, but—"

"You're fired, MacPherson. Stop by the front office and pick up your severance pay. I don't ever want to see you around here again, understand?" Before the man could say another word, Pappas was gone.

Mattie and Nancy looked at each other. "You've got to believe me," Mattie whispered urgently. "That was no accident, I'm sure of it!"

Nancy sighed. If security thought it was an accident, it probably was. Still . . . "I think I'll take a look around myself. You never know."

There wasn't much to see. All the glass from the broken light had been swept into a pile in the corner, and the light itself was in pieces against the wall. Each piece had been tagged for reference. Security seemed to have done a thorough job.

Nancy was about to give up and go back to Rick's dressing room but decided to take a last look around. As she walked over to the back wall of the living room, a flash of something metallic caught her eye, and she bent to the floor. There, almost completely hidden from view, was a piece of metal with a bolt attached. One edge of the metal was shiny, as if it had been scraped or cut.

Nancy walked over to the lighting technician, who was gloomily gathering his things together. "Excuse me," she said, "but—could I ask you a question?"

The man turned around and looked at her for a moment. "Oh, hi, I remember you. You're the girl who saved Rick's life," he said with a smile. "I guess I should thank you. I'd have been in *real* trouble if he'd gotten hurt."

"You don't have to thank me," Nancy waved him off. "But you could tell me what this is." She showed him the bolt she'd found.

"Why, that's a C-clamp. They're used to hold the lights on the bar."

"Does it look odd to you? Is there anything strange about it?"

MacPherson studied the clamp briefly. "One end's been sawed," he gasped. "Almost clean through. The rest looks like it snapped off. This must be— But if—"

"Just what I was thinking," Nancy said, agreeing. "That was no accident this morning. The light was rigged so it would fall. Somebody tried to kill Rick Arlen—and almost succeeded!"

Chapter Four

"Do you believe me *now?*" Mattie was on the verge of tears as she pleaded with the chief of security. She and Nancy had just shown him the broken clamp. "I've been telling people for weeks that someone was after Rick, but nobody believed me. You've got to believe me now!"

"Now, Mattie," Pappas said, patting his leading lady on the arm. "Let's not get hysterical and blow this out of proportion."

"Well, I'll be," the security man muttered as he examined the C-clamp. "Where exactly did you say you found this, young lady?"

"By the back wall of the set," Nancy replied.

"Well, it proves the light was sabotaged. No doubt about it."

"This is just what I need," Pappas muttered in frustration. "I don't have enough problems without someone sabotaging my show!"

"Mr. Pappas, who actually has access to this stage?" the chief wanted to know.

"Well, the crew and the actors, of course. Nobody else, really. Maybe an occasional guest, but they all register at the front desk."

"Wasn't there a tour group in here earlier today?" Nancy asked.

Pappas snapped his fingers. "Right!"

"And some of them were mad at Rory Danner, too," Nancy said.

"You don't suppose some crazy fan could have—" Pappas shook his head.

"There're a lot of nuts out there, Mr. Pappas," the chief said. "All it takes is one person who can't tell fantasy from reality."

"That settles it!" Pappas exclaimed. "From now on this set is closed to anyone not directly involved in the show." Yelling across the studio, Pappas repeated his order for everyone to hear. "That means no guests, no agents, no mothers, fathers, sisters, or brothers. I want this set sealed tighter than a pharaoh's tomb!

"Now, we'll take a couple-hour break and then back to work. If you need anything, I'll be in my office."

After Pappas walked away, Nancy turned toward Mattie.

"Thank goodness he gave us a break," she told Nancy. "I've got to go rest." Rubbing her eyes, she added, "See you later. And thanks again for saving Rick's life." Flashing Nancy a grateful smile, Mattie walked off the set.

Since the set was closed to guests, Nancy and Bess had to leave. Nancy began to make her way back toward Rick's dressing room to collect Bess. But she soon realized she must have gone through the wrong door or made a wrong turn somewhere. One long corridor led to another, and for a moment Nancy didn't know which way to turn. Then the sound of a door slowly opening caught her attention. Instinctively knowing that she shouldn't be there, Nancy moved back into a recessed doorway and waited silently.

Nancy could just see Lillian Weiss nervously looking both ways before stepping into the hall. Once the door was closed behind her, Lillian seemed to relax. Nancy's heart was in her throat as she realized Lillian was heading straight for her. Nancy opened the door behind her and slammed it, making it sound as if she had just come through that door. She stepped out into the corridor.

"Well, well," Lillian said, greeting Nancy with a snarl. "Is our fair rescuer lost and helpless?"

"Yes, I guess I am. I was looking for Rick's dressing room, actually," Nancy told her. Well, it was almost the truth.

"Continue down this corridor and make your first left," Lillian snapped. "And by the way, it was nice knowing you. I'm sure now that Pappas has closed the set, you won't be around anymore. Too bad. I'm sure you were Rick's favorite little bodyguard." With a smug smile, Lillian continued down the hall and disappeared around a corner.

The room that Lillian had come out of turned out to be the prop room. After making sure she was alone, Nancy ventured inside.

At first she was overwhelmed by what she saw. The room was huge, with several long aisles. Stacked from floor to ceiling, making an incredible clutter, were thousands upon thousands of items—anything that could ever possibly be needed on the set of the show. As organized as the room seemed to be, with everything numbered and labeled, there was no way to keep it all neat. Dust covered some of the items that hadn't been used recently, and Nancy felt her nose begin to itch.

There seemed to be nobody there, but when Nancy sneezed, she heard a rustling in a far corner. A copy of the *Daily News* moved, and a grizzled head poked out from under it. The old man had a mop of unruly white hair flowing out from an ancient orange cap.

"Who's there?" a crackly voice called. "I'm awake, I'm awake. On the job all the time, yessir! What can I do for you?"

Nancy couldn't help smiling at the wizened old man. He wore red suspenders, which held up a pair of baggy gray pants, and he was covered with as much dust as everything else in the room. Nancy would have almost believed that he had been sleeping there uninterrupted for years.

"Sorry, I must have opened the wrong door," she said, apologizing.

"Oh, it's good to have a little company," the man said. "This week has been just kitchen stuff and living room knickknacks, day after day. I've been sitting here reading my paper all week without seeing a soul."

"But wasn't the assistant director in here just a moment ago?" Nancy said.

"Who? Lillian? Nah, haven't seen Lillian in ages. The only time she ever came into the prop room was to complain that a butcher knife didn't look sharp enough. I had to put a little oil on it to give it that threatening gleam when the camera panned in on it. That's an old prop man's trick, you know."

"Achoo!" Nancy couldn't help sneezing again. "Are you sure no one was in here earlier?" she asked again, persisting.

"Absolutely one hundred percent, young lady. And nobody gets anything by me."

That's what you think, Nancy thought as she said goodbye to the prop man. As she stepped back into the corridor and made her way to Rick's dressing room, Nancy's mind was in a whirl. Maybe one of the fans from the tour group *had* tampered with the klieg light. She supposed it was possible. But even so, something funny was definitely going on. What had Lillian been doing in the prop room? And why was she so hostile? Nancy was determined to find out. And that meant she had to get onto the set again the next day and do some more checking around.

Here I am, she said to herself as she turned a corner and saw the familiar door with the star on it. Wait till I tell Bess what I found!

A moment later, after a quick knock, she threw open the door, smiling broadly. What she saw made her stop dead. Bess was in Rick's arms, and they looked about a split second away from a kiss too steamy for TV!

Chapter Five

NANCY!" BESS CRIED, awkwardly trying to disentangle herself from Rick's embrace.

Nancy looked from a blushing Bess to Rick and back, "I'm sorry to interrupt, but—"

"It's not what you think!" Bess said, interrupting her as she tossed her blond hair over her shoulder and straightened her collar. "Rick just asked me to help him rehearse, that's all."

"She's very talented," Rick said, putting his arm around Bess's waist and drawing her closer.

"Well, I just came to tell you that Pappas

closed the set to all visitors," Nancy said, looking at Bess.

But Bess wasn't about to let anything ruin her day. "Nancy, you'll never guess what Rick has offered to do!"

"It's really nothing," Rick said, protesting.

"Nothing?" Bess replied, her eyes dancing with excitement. "You call taking me all over the city in a limousine nothing?"

"Well, I already have the limousine." Rick shrugged modestly.

"He's going to give me a personal tour of the city on Saturday! Would you believe he's never been on top of the Empire State Building?"

"How can you live in New York and not visit the Empire State Building?" Nancy asked.

"Actually, a lot of New Yorkers have never been there," he explained. "We always say we're going to go someday, but somehow we never get around to it. It'll be a real treat for me."

Bess continued to gaze at the handsome TV star. Nancy couldn't help worrying that her friend might be getting in over her head.

"Bess, aren't you forgetting that Rick might be in danger? I don't know if it's such a great idea for you to be alone with him, you know."

"Don't be silly!" Rick laughed, wiping his makeup off with a thick cloth. "I can take care of both of us. Listen, I've got an even better idea—why don't you come, too? I'm sure I could round up a friend for you."

"That's great!" Bess cried happily, turning to Nancy.

"Okay, count me in," Nancy agreed. Spending the day with Rick was one way to keep an eye on him. And on Bess.

"Come on, Bess," she said, taking her friend by the elbow. "We'd better leave the set. Nice meeting you, Rick." Nancy turned to the door, but Bess wasn't quite finished talking to Rick.

"Well, I'm sorry we have to go so soon, but we're definitely on for Saturday, aren't we?" she asked.

"I can hardly wait, love," he replied, blowing her a kiss. "Till then, 'Parting is such sweet sorrow.'"

As soon as she closed the door, Bess stood stock-still for a moment. Then she leaned on the wall in a daze. "Did you hear? He called me 'love.'"

"I heard," Nancy replied uneasily.

"Oh, Nancy," Bess cooed, "he's so wonderful! Not at all conceited like some big stars probably are. Just think, I have a date with *the* Rick Arlen. Me—Bess Marvin, regular person! Do you know how many girls would kill for a date with the star of 'Danner's Dream'?"

"Yeah—" Nancy said, only half paying attention. She was wondering who was trying to kill Rick Arlen—and why?

"We were standing there, watching this intense scene. I mean, it was so quiet you could hear your heart beating!" Bess was going over the whole day as Nancy's aunt emptied a package of white mushrooms into her food processor. "And then, well, the light just snapped! Right in front of our eyes! Right, Nancy?"

Nancy looked up from the microwave, where she was getting ready to bake three potatoes. "Uh-huh," she agreed.

"And Nancy saved the day. You should have seen her," Bess said, continuing. "I don't know how she reacted so fast. The light only missed him by a few inches. And Rick is amazing. He wasn't even afraid! He said it was all in a day's work. Can you believe it?"

Eloise's eyes clouded over with worry. "I'm not sure I want you two poking around in a place where they have accidents like that," she said, shaking her head.

Nancy looked over at Bess and put her finger on her lips, but Bess didn't pick up on it.

"Oh, no!" Bess went on. "It *wasn't* an accident! Nancy found the evidence—somebody tampered with the light!"

"Nancy!" Aunt Eloise exclaimed. "Do you mean to say Mattie was right to suspect something was wrong? Oh, dear, please be careful! I don't want you getting hurt."

Bess laughed and shook her head. "Don't worry, Rick says it's just some crazy fan trying to scare him. Now that they've closed the set, I'm sure there won't be any more trouble."

Just then the phone rang.

"Hello?" Eloise answered. "Oh, yes, Mattie, we're here. Come on up." Replacing the receiver, she said, "I hope it's all right if Mattie joins us. I should have asked you first."

"It's fine with me!" Bess cried happily.

Nancy went to the vegetable bin and took out another potato. After rinsing it, she popped it into the microwave.

"That's it," Eloise said. "Dinner in ten minutes."

In a few minutes there was a knock on the door, and Nancy went to open it.

"Hi, everybody!" Mattie called as she breezed into the apartment with a bouquet of spring flowers. Nancy was amazed at how carefree Mattie seemed. "Oh, I'm so happy you're on the case," she cried, embracing Nancy warmly. "I know nothing bad can happen to Rick now."

Nancy frowned slightly. Everyone seemed to think Rick Arlen was safe, including Rick himself. She wasn't at all convinced.

"Did you hear about your niece, this morning's heroine?" Mattie said, going over to kiss

Eloise and hand her the flowers. "You weren't exaggerating when you told me how brave she was."

Eloise reddened and looked over at Nancy. "Don't get the wrong idea," she warned. "I'm proud of you, but that doesn't mean I approve of your taking unnecessary risks. Please be careful."

"I will," Nancy promised.

Dinner was ready, and the four of them gathered around the large oak table in the dining area.

"Marinated steak. Smells great, and I don't mind saying so myself," Eloise remarked. "I may not be the greatest cook, but every once in a while I do all right."

"I can testify personally that she's a fantastic cook," Mattie said with a laugh. After they ate and chatted for a while, Mattie turned more serious and asked, "So, Nancy, what do you think? Was it someone from the tour group who tampered with the light?"

"Well, some people seem to think that," Nancy answered. "But from what I can tell, his fans aren't the only ones who're angry at Rick. There are other people—people who see him every day. Pappas, for instance. Or Lillian Weiss. Maybe others, too."

"Hah! You don't know the half of it," Mattie said. "There isn't a person on that set who Rick hasn't alienated at one time or another."

"Really? Why?" Nancy wondered.

"Oh, Rick's just— He's talented, handsome, and rich. Some people would hate him just for that, but he's also walked over a lot of people to get where he is. He's used a lot of people, broken a lot of hearts—" She sighed deeply.

Was one of those broken hearts Mattie's? Nancy wondered. The actress seemed so fragile and sad when she talked about Rick.

"I wish I could point to just one person and say, 'That's the one,' but Rick has made a lot of enemies." Mattie shook her head and reached for her glass of mineral water.

"People resent his success," Bess commented. "He was telling me about that today, about how jealous people are of him. How they all want something from him."

"Oh," Mattie said, turning to face Bess. "You two were talking together?"

"Uh-huh!" Bess said happily. "We found out we have a lot in common."

"I see," Mattie said, looking down at her plate.

"Wait a minute," Bess said slowly. "You two aren't going out or anything, are you?"

"Oh, no," Mattie quickly replied. "That is, not anymore."

So, Mattie *was* one of those broken hearts! Nancy thought.

"Oh, phew." Bess breathed a sigh of relief.

"I wouldn't want to steal somebody else's boyfriend or anything. You see, he's asked me out for Saturday."

"He—he asked you out?" Mattie whispered. Her eyes grew incredibly wide, and her mouth fell open.

"Yes," Nancy interjected soothingly. "And I'm going along, too. It's perfect, don't you think? That way I can keep an eye on Rick."

"I see." Mattie looked somewhat calmed by Nancy's explanation. Still, she turned to Bess with a sudden, compelling stare. "Just be careful, please," she said, warning her. "You don't know Rick the way I do—you don't know how dangerous he can be."

Chapter Six

"LISTEN, BESS—" MATTIE relaxed her stare a bit, trying hard not to look so severe. "I really don't want to upset you, but, honestly, Rick can really love them and leave them. Maybe it's because deep down inside, he's very unsure of himself. Or maybe he's become too successful too fast, and— Sometimes I wonder if he can really handle it."

"Rick? Unsure of himself?" Bess shook her head in disbelief. "I'm sorry, Mattie. I don't think you know the real Rick."

"Maybe not, but I've known him a long time. We did summer stock together years ago.

He was different then, warm and sincere. In the past few years, he's really changed. He can be so cold now, even cruel."

"Well, maybe he just hasn't met the right girl yet," Bess suggested.

"Wait a minute," Nancy interrupted. "Mattie, why are you so concerned about a man you've just told us is cold, cruel, and steps on people?"

"Oh, I don't know," Mattie answered softly. "I guess I still think of him as a friend, even if it didn't work out between us." Looking over at Nancy imploringly, she added, "Rick would never admit it, but I'm sure that way down deep he's scared. I'd just feel so much better if you were on the set tomorrow."

Bess rolled her eyes and got up from the table. Nancy watched her go. She hoped Bess knew what she was doing where Rick was concerned.

"I'd like to be there myself," Nancy replied, turning back to Mattie. "But now that the set's closed to visitors—"

"Wait a minute!" Mattie cried. Her eyes shimmered with excitement. "I just got a brilliant idea! We're shooting a hospital scene tomorrow, and I'll bet I could get you and Bess jobs as extras! What do you think? Will you do it?"

Across the kitchen, Bess couldn't help jumping up and down with excitement. "That would be fantastic!"

Nancy thought for a moment. "Are you sure you could do it?"

"Almost sure. Here, let me call the casting director. Eloise, do you have a phone book handy?"

Nancy's aunt brought the book over as Bess loaded the dishwasher. "Just imagine, Nancy, appearing on my favorite soap!"

"We're in luck!" Mattie announced, hanging up the phone a few minutes later. "She says you two can be nurses. Just report to the studio at seven sharp, and go straight to the costume room as soon as you get there."

"But what if people recognize us?" Nancy wondered out loud.

"Oh, they won't recognize you." Mattie laughed and stood up to leave. "No one ever looks at the extras. Besides, when you're on camera you'll probably have wigs and uniforms on. You probably won't even recognize yourselves."

"You know, Nancy," Bess said after Mattie had gone. "No matter what anyone says, I've read that a lot of big stars started out as extras. You never know—this could be my lucky break!"

Bess and Nancy had reported to the studio at seven the next morning. After the dry blocking, in which they learned what they were to do, they reported to makeup and wardrobe. Now, standing on pedestals as two wardrobe people finished their final fittings for the dress rehearsal, Bess and Nancy couldn't help giggling.

"You're really a knockout as a brunette, Nancy!" Bess said.

Nancy looked over at her friend, who was wearing an identical uniform. She had a white nurse's cap over her bright red wig, and Nancy had never seen her look more excited.

"Your dress rehearsal will be third, ladies," a production assistant told them. "After the big love scene, which is the second, report to Lillian. You know where to stand and what to do from the first rehearsal. So, break a leg. Oh, if you want to catch Rick and Mattie in rehearsal, you can. Rory and Serena are going to have a big scene. It's supposed to be pretty hot stuff."

Bess immediately dashed down the corridor to the set, determined not to miss a word of Mattie and Rick's scene. It was all Nancy could do to keep up with her.

Watching the cast and crew gather around the set of Serena Livingstone's living room, Nancy could feel their edginess. The near-disaster of the day before had obviously gotten to everyone. Even though the set was closed to outsiders, Nancy could tell that nobody felt truly safe.

The only person who seemed at ease was Rick. Flashing a smile at Bess as he walked onto the set, he looked as if he were on top of the world.

He took his place in the middle of the set, and slowly Rick Arlen seemed to fade away. When the director finally called "Action," he had become Rory Danner.

In the scene, Rory was supposed to tell Serena that he'd be hers forever, if she would have him. Even though it was an intense scene, Nancy noticed that Rick was reading nearly all his lines from the teleprompter. But then, with all the excitement the day before, she reasoned, he probably hadn't had time to memorize them.

Mattie was having trouble with her lines, too. She had excused herself early the night before to go home and work, but obviously she didn't remember much. Although she was really throwing herself into the scene, Nancy noticed that she, too, kept glancing over at her teleprompter to check her lines.

"Should I leave, Serena? Is that what you want?" Rick asked, pacing in front of Mattie nervously.

"No, Rory, don't go. I love you," Serena said. Her voice was quivering, and her emerald eyes were full of tears. "I've always loved you, even when you didn't want me."

"Cut!" came the director's voice. "Mattie, I need you to cool it a little. If you start the scene at such a high emotional pitch, we won't have anywhere to go."

"Right, Luther." Mattie nodded up to the director's booth.

"Okay, everyone, take it from 'Should I leave,'" Lillian ordered.

"Should I leave, Serena? Is that what you want?" Rick said.

"No, Rory, don't go. I love you! I've always loved you, even when you didn't want me."

They were into it by then. Mattie and Rick were utterly convincing, making everyone who was watching really believe they were desperately in love. Bess had tears in her eyes as she watched them move slowly toward each other. Finally, Serena collapsed in Rory's arms.

"Here comes her big speech," Lillian muttered under her breath to nobody in particular. "Watch her screw it up."

"Oh, Rory, I want to do so many things with you," Mattie whispered hoarsely. "I want to take walks in the rain with you, I want to sit with you under the stars on a deserted beach. I want to dance with you, to sing with you, to—"

Mattie suddenly fell silent. She stood as if frozen, her eyes fixed on the teleprompter, her beautiful face a terrible white. Then, as everyone looked on in horror, she let out a bloodcurdling scream and slumped slowly to the floor.

Chapter Seven

"MATTIE! MATTIE!"

"What happened?"

"Is she all right?"

"Don't touch her!"

Everyone gathered around Mattie, who was lying on the floor. After what seemed forever, her eyes began to flutter open. She looked dazed. Mattie struggled to her feet with Rick's help. The look in her eyes only grew wilder.

"Look!" she cried, pointing to the teleprompter.

Her monologue had been changed. It read: "I WANT TO DANCE WITH YOU, TO SING WITH YOU,

TO MURDER YOU. YES, YOUR TIME IS UP, RICK ARLEN. I'M GOING TO KILL YOU. I'M GOING TO WATCH YOU DIE A HORRIBLE DEATH, AND I'M GOING TO LAUGH."

"What in the name of— What is this?" Pappas yelled. "Get me the teleprompter operator! I want to talk to her right now!"

"I'm here, Mr. Pappas." A short red-haired girl spoke up.

"Would you care to explain this?" he asked, arching his eyebrows.

"Well, sir, I, uh—I really can't explain it," the girl stammered. "I got here early to type in the scene, and I was at the keyboard all morning. The only time I left was to take a phone call. And I know I wasn't gone for more than a minute because when I picked up the phone, there was no one there. I—I didn't think—"

"Exactly, you didn't think." Pappas shot the operator a harsh look. "You're fired. And whoever's job it was to keep strangers off this set, you're fired, too." Then, to the frightened cast and crew he said, "I'll fire every last one of you if I have to. This nonsense has got to stop!"

Nancy watched the producer from the sidelines. He seemed genuinely concerned, but what if it was all an act? What if beneath all his theatrics, there was something completely different going on, something much more calculated—and sinister?

She noticed Lillian Weiss, too. Lillian was off in a corner, trying to be inconspicuous, but nothing could hide the pleased look on her face. She was loving every minute of all this.

"Okay, everybody," Luther's voice boomed from the director's booth. "Lunch break. And when we come back, let's try to get this show back on schedule, shall we?"

"Calm down, Mattie! You're not going to let some practical joker ruin your day, are you?" Rick opened the front door of the studio for them, and Mattie, Bess, and Nancy filed past him onto the sidewalk.

"Come on," he added with a grin. "Let me treat you all to lunch—while I'm still alive, that is."

"Stop it! Stop pretending everything's fine!" Mattie turned on him, her green eyes flashing. "You've got to be terrified! Why don't you just come out and admit it?"

"Me? Terrified? Don't be ridiculous—they can't kill me. The world needs me! Besides, it'd spoil the ratings if I died."

"Oh, I could just punch you," Mattie growled. "And I'll pay for my own lunch, thank you."

"Whatever you say." Rick shrugged. "I'll just have to treat Bess—and Nancy, of course. Right, ladies?"

Bess and Nancy said nothing, embarrassed

by the way Rick was taunting Mattie. Nancy started to walk off by herself.

"Hey, look who's here!" said Rick, his attention caught by a man at the studio door. "It's the president of the losers' league himself. Hi, Dwayne."

Dwayne Casper, Mattie's agent, rushed up to them, pointedly ignoring Rick's remark. Nancy stopped and observed the scene at a short distance from the others. "Mattie!" he cried, throwing his arms around her. "I was bringing some of your new head shots to the front office and I heard what happened. It's absolutely outrageous! Are you all right, darling?"

"Oh, I suppose so," Mattie replied softly, shaking free of his embrace. "It was awfully upsetting, but—"

"But nothing," Dwayne said, interrupting. "You're in danger, and I won't have it!"

"Keep your shirt on, Casper," Rick said, with a scornful laugh. "This nut is supposedly after me, not Mattie. Why don't you leave us alone and go hover over some of your other clients. If you have any, that is."

"Rick!" Mattie cried sharply.

"It's all right, Mattie, he doesn't bother me. As long as you're all right—"

"I'm fine, Dwayne. Please don't worry about me." Mattie smiled at him warmly. "Honest."

"Yeah, don't worry, old buddy. I'll take care of Mattie," Rick said, trying to assure him.

"Oh, I'm sure you will." Dwayne sneered. Then he turned to Mattie and took her by the hand, looking deeply into her eyes. "I want you to promise to call me if there's any more trouble on the set."

Mattie nodded, then Dwayne walked off, throwing a nasty look over his shoulder at Rick.

"For pete's sake, Mattie," Rick muttered before Dwayne was out of earshot, "when are you going to dump that jerk and get yourself a real agent!"

"Oh, Dwayne's not so bad," Mattie answered, watching the man disappear. "Remember, he took me on as a client when nobody else would even give me an interview."

"But you've come a long way since then. You're a star now. You should have a major agency representing you," he said as they started walking to catch up with Nancy.

"I don't know. Somehow I'd feel like a rat if I left Dwayne."

"All I know is, a major agency could get you a lot more work and more money. And a girl with your talent deserves the best." Seeing he was getting nowhere, Rick threw up his hands. "All right, I won't say another word. You know how I feel, though." He stopped in front of an expensive-looking restaurant. "Here we are. Serena, Nurse Sanford, Nurse Johnson, would you care to have lunch with me?" he said, opening the restaurant door for them.

"It's Saturday morning and time for another edition of 'Soap Opera Weekly,' where we bring you the latest on your favorite shows and introduce you to the stars," the television announcer was saying as Bess shook Nancy's shoulder.

"Wake up, Nancy Drew!" Bess said, mimicking the announcer. "Come on. The alarm went off ten minutes ago! Your aunt's still sleeping so I wheeled the TV in here. Rick's going to be on 'Soap Opera Weekly' this morning. We can watch while we get dressed."

"Mumpfh—" Nancy mumbled, burying her head under the pillow. Was it really morning already?

She and Bess and her aunt Eloise had had such a great time the night before. They'd gone to see *Soft Shoe,* the Broadway musical smash of the season. The show was wonderful, but they'd stopped for a bite to eat afterward. By the time they got home, it was almost one in the morning.

Flipping over and squinting at the TV, Nancy saw shots of different soap opera stars as the upbeat theme song played in the background.

"Our special 'Soap Opera Weekly' guest today is the star of 'Danner's Dream'!" the announcer said. "Will he and Serena Livingstone finally tie the knot this time? Mr. Sex Appeal himself, Rick Arlen, will be here with us in just a few minutes! But first—"

The commercial came on, and Nancy realized there was no way she was going to get back to sleep. Not with Bess rummaging around the room, tossing one outfit after another on the bed and saying things like, "What do you think, Nancy? The pink or the yellow?"

Pulling herself up onto her elbows, Nancy yawned and looked out the window. It was a glorious day outside—warm and sunny. A perfect day for seeing the sights, she thought happily.

"He's on! He's on!" Bess shouted a few minutes later. Nancy turned from the closet and saw Rick. He was seated casually across from the interviewer, waving and nodding as the audience clapped and cheered.

Cleverly refusing to give away any of the show's carefully guarded secrets, Rick did admit that he was considering leaving the show at the end of the season to star in a movie. The audience groaned, then applauded.

"Tell us about the real Rick Arlen," the interviewer prompted. "Could we be hearing wedding bells soon?"

Laughing, Rick made an old joke about the gossip columns having him engaged to three different girls. "But then, you never can tell," he added slyly, blowing a kiss to a "special lady out there."

"He means me!" Bess cried happily.

"I don't think so. That's just talk, Bess. He could mean anybody—or nobody."

Bess shot her friend an angry scowl, and Nancy decided to back off.

After the interview with Rick, the show moved on to an update of that network's daytime and evening soap operas. Bess snapped the TV off then.

"He said he'd be here in an hour. I can't wait!" Bess scooped up her makeup and headed for the bathroom. "Hey, I wonder who he'll bring for you, Nancy. I mean, any friend of Rick's is probably cute, but I wonder what he'll be like."

An hour later the apartment intercom buzzed, signaling the arrival of Rick and his limousine.

Bess checked herself in the mirror one last time. She looked terrific in an oversize cotton cardigan and flowing skirt and flats. "Not bad," she pronounced. "Come on, Nancy!" With that, she flew down the steps of the brownstone to the waiting limousine.

"Not bad at all," Nancy admitted, looking admiringly at Rick's limo. The uniformed driver ushered them into the backseat, where Rick was waiting.

"Good morning, girls!" he said brightly. "Welcome to my abode on the road."

The first order of business was to pick up Rick's friend, a guy named Gilbert Frost. "He's an old pal from acting school," Rick explained. "You'll love him."

Bess threw Nancy a meaningful look, but Nancy just sighed and looked out the window. There was no way that she was going to fall for any of Rick Arlen's friends—not when she was in love with Ned Nickerson. Of course, Ned would understand her being on this date —she had to go. Someone's life was in jeopardy.

At the corner of Twenty-third Street and Park Avenue South, she noticed a skinny guy in jeans and running shoes, leaning against a streetlight. He looked totally normal, except that he was wearing big black-rimmed glasses and a false nose.

"What?" Nancy mumbled as the limo stopped in front of him. The man swept down in a low courtly bow.

"Hey there, Gil!" Rick laughed, opening the door. "Girls, I'd like you to meet Gilbert Frost. Say hello, Gilbert."

"Hello, Gilbert!" the guy mimicked, sliding into the plush limo.

Bess was giggling uncontrollably, and Nancy

couldn't help smiling as Rick's friend took off his glasses, revealing another pair underneath.

Finally, they pulled back into traffic and Nancy got a good look at Gilbert. Without his getup on, he was pretty cute. He had glossy black hair and warm brown eyes that twinkled with laughter.

"Gil is going to be the next host at the Comedy Basement," Rick said. "He does stand-up."

"I also do sit up and grow up," Gil announced. Everyone groaned.

Throwing a proprietary arm around Bess's shoulder, Rick instructed the driver to take them to Forty-second Street and the Hudson River.

"Today we're going to do all those corny things you see in old movies about New York," Rick said. "Like go on a boat trip around Manhattan and to the top of the Empire State Building. Bess is a very old-fashioned girl," he explained to his friend.

"Rick Arlen! I am *not!*" Bess protested. Secretly, though, she was flattered by his remark.

By the time they got to the West Side pier, the four of them were relaxed and having a great time. Before leaving the limo, Rick put on sunglasses and an old hat. That way, most of his face was covered. "Just normal precautions," he insisted. "These go everywhere with me. Otherwise, the fans—well, I'm sure you can imagine."

"I think you look adorable like that," Gilbert said. Rick punched his friend lightly on the arm, and they all piled out of the car.

"So, Gil, how did you get involved in show business?" Nancy asked while they waited on deck for the cruise to start.

"Oh, now we're going way back—to the day little Freddie Gilbert was born in Illinois in a log cabin— No, no, just kidding. How did I get involved in show business, you ask. Thank goodness someone cares besides my mother."

In spite of his nonstop chatter and putdown humor, Nancy decided she liked Gil. He seemed a little lonely, somehow, and afraid to be just himself, but instinct told her he had a good heart.

"You see, my real name is Fred Gilbert. I had to change it after I got to New York. There already was a Fred Gilbert out there in the show business stratosphere. And so Gilbert Frost was born. But he had the wrong nose. So I changed that, too. And then I had to darken my hair. By the time I was finished, the same club owners who used to tell me to get lost were dying to sign me. What can I tell you? It's a crazy business. Maybe someday I'll even make enough to pay my rent. And if I'm really lucky, I might even hit it big like old Rick here."

"I'm sure you will," Nancy said, looking up. The view from the boat was spectacular—the skyline sparkled in the noon sun.

But as the boat trip continued and they finally circled the northern tip of Manhattan, Nancy couldn't help feeling that something was wrong. All through the ride, she had been keeping an eye on Rick. And she noticed other people were watching him, too. Nancy saw two women look at him, jab each other, and whisper. And a child tugged on his father's sleeve and pointed toward Rick. A portly man was also watching him, although he pretended to be looking at something else.

As the boat swung into the final leg of the tour, Nancy recognized the portly man. He had been the one cursing Rory Danner on the tour of the set just two days before.

"Attention, ladies and gentlemen. We will be docking in a few minutes. Please disembark via the white stairs on the port side of the boat. That's the left, to all you landlubbers," the tour guide instructed.

"That's him! That's Rick Arlen!" a young woman suddenly shrieked.

An excited murmur went through the crowd, and everyone turned to look at Rick.

"Take the hat off, Rory! We know it's you!" a woman called out good-naturedly. The group laughed, and Rick cooperated.

"Ah, my fans." He smiled and waved.

"You're the greatest—all of you! I love you madly!"

"Rick, may I have your autograph?" a woman cried happily. Everyone crowded around him and began rifling through their bags for pens, too.

"Write one for my niece, Rick!"

"Oh, Mr. Arlen, thank you!"

Rick was standing by the guardrail signing the backs of envelopes, napkins, address books, and matchbook covers. Suddenly, the man who had been on the studio tour lunged forward, his eyes wild, his voice like thunder. "You killed Jill Rowan, and now you want to destroy Serena Livingstone. Well, I won't let you! I'm not going to let filth like you near her! You're going to die, Rory Danner—right now!"

With that, the man lunged for Rick, sending him halfway over the rail. He was about to plunge into the river!

Chapter Eight

LEAPING FOR RICK, Nancy and Gilbert grabbed him just in time and pulled him safely back over the rail. Nancy felt a pair of hamlike hands on her shoulders. She turned to face the assailant and delivered a swift kick to his left shin. Then she seized his hand and flipped him head over heels onto the deck. The ship's crew then held him pinned against the deck until the ship had docked and the police arrived, followed by a couple of reporters.

"Okay, fella, let's go," a police officer said, leading the man to a patrol car. "You'll feel a lot better after a nice long rest."

"I killed Rory Danner and the world will be a better place for it!" the man exclaimed. "He was filth! Filth!"

"Sure, sure," another police officer said, agreeing. "You can tell the doctor all about it."

As their limo pulled out of the parking lot, the crowd cheered Rick. He was leaning out the window, smiling and waving.

"Thank you, everyone!" he called. He slipped back into the car. "Well, thank goodness that's over. And thank you, Gil. And Nancy." Turning to Bess, he added, "You certainly know how to pick your friends, love."

Gil still seemed a bit shaken. "You know, Rick, the way you were hanging over the edge there, I thought you were history." He shuddered. "I'm going to sign up for karate lessons next week. I want to be prepared for fame."

"Let's just put the whole thing behind us, okay? Now it's time to celebrate!" Rick grinned devilishly. "Why not go for the best! Driver—take us to Trump Tower!"

Later, riding up the escalator from the lobby of the brass-and-marble palace, Bess and Nancy looked around in wonder. The place was amazing!

"This makes the River Heights mall look

like a mom-and-pop store," Nancy whispered. She looked all around her as they rose ever higher through the glittering atrium.

"Tell me about it!" Bess said enthusiastically. "Rick, I can't believe people actually *live* in this building."

"They do," he assured her. "There are apartments here that sell for millions."

"Seriously?" Bess couldn't believe it. "What do they have, solid gold faucets?"

"Almost," Gil replied. "You'd be amazed at what people spend their money on."

"Cappuccino, anyone?" Rick broke in cheerfully. They had just come to an attractive café on an upper level.

Soon they were all sitting around a table sipping cups of the strong Italian coffee.

"You know what being here makes me realize?" Bess was saying. "I've realized that I'd make a great millionaire."

"I think you'd make a lovely one, too," Rick said, flirting. "In fact, I saw something in a shop across the way that I think you should have. Be right back."

A minute later Rick came back to the table, holding a silk scarf printed in pastel geometric shapes. It matched Bess's outfit perfectly.

"Oh, Rick!" she exclaimed. "It's beautiful!"

"Wear it and think of me," he murmured. "So, everyone, are you ready to scale the heights? It's such a clear beautiful day—what do you say we catch the view from the Empire State Building?"

"Sounds great!" Bess was beaming. Anything Rick said would have sounded great to her.

"I used to sell souvenirs at the observatory," Gil threw in. "That was when I still *worked* for a living." He straightened up and helped Nancy from her chair. "Madame?" he said. "Your chariot awaits. That is, *Rick's* chariot awaits," he said, correcting himself.

By the time they reached Thirty-fourth Street and made their way up to the top, the sun had slipped much closer to the horizon. Rick and Bess, their arms around each other's waists, stood at the observatory's edge, gazing into the distance. Gil had stopped to chat with his old coworkers at the souvenir shop, so Nancy wandered off by herself.

Up that high, the wind cut like a knife, seeming to come from all directions. It blew Nancy's hair wildly around her as she stared down at the magical city. The noise from the street sounded like a low moan up there, almost human and full of sadness. It made Nancy shudder for a moment.

As she looked out over the city below her, she felt a growing sense of dread. The police had arrested the deranged fan that afternoon, but she was still worried. In the late afternoon sun, Nancy had a sudden, powerful feeling that someone *else* was after Rick. Someone who was not only crazy, but also clever, determined, and deadly. Nancy felt an icy shiver go through her. Someone was waiting down on the street—she was sure of it—waiting to end Rick Arlen's life.

Bess scooped up one last mouthful of chocolate mousse pie and sighed contentedly. "What a dinner! I'm in heaven."

"Not bad," Gil agreed, glancing around at the glass walls of Tavern on the Green. Positioned on the edge of Central Park, the view out the windows of the restaurant was of trees decorated with tiny white lights. The park looked like an enchanted fairyland, in direct contrast to the city around it.

When the check came, Rick picked it up. "What's money for if not to treat friends?" he asked, placing a gold credit card on the small black lacquered tray the waiter had brought.

"What a day!" Bess remarked happily. "What a night, too! I've had such a fabulous time today, Rick . . . thanks to you."

Rick looked genuinely pleased as he took her hand in his. "There's just one more thing I'd like to do. I could use a little exercise after this dinner, and it's such a great night—why don't we take a walk beside the park?"

Bess's eyes were twinkling with delight. Rick

seemed to be having a hard time saying good night to her!

"A walk sounds wonderful," Nancy said.

"Good, we're on!" Gil agreed.

Stepping out onto the sidewalk along the park, Rick and Bess linked arms. They were completely caught up in each other as they giggled and joked, walking ahead of the other two. Nancy watched them carefully as she half listened to Gil, who was telling her the rest of his life story.

"Then I realized I had to change my material," he was saying. "Nobody goes for rubber-chicken jokes anymore. So I began writing myself a whole new act. . . ."

Nancy couldn't help worrying about Bess. She was heading for trouble, Nancy was sure of that. Even if Rick was sincere, how could it last? They lived miles from each other. And a broken heart was the last thing Bess needed.

The sound of a speeding car made Nancy spin around. A taxicab jumped its lane and screeched diagonally across the street. Suddenly a broken heart was the least of Bess's troubles. The out-of-control cab was headed onto the sidewalk, aimed straight at Rick —and Bess!

Chapter Nine

"WATCH OUT!" NANCY screamed. Racing up to pull Bess away from the oncoming taxi, she managed to get just close enough to grab her friend's arm as the taxi swerved onto the sidewalk. It barely missed the stunned Bess before jumping the curb back onto the street and careening away.

Bess stood absolutely still in the middle of the sidewalk. "Nancy? Am I okay?" she asked in a dazed voice.

"Your shirt is torn, but I think you're fine."

Suddenly Bess looked around frantically. "Rick! Where's Rick?"

"Right here," he answered. They all turned

and saw Rick's head poking out from behind a tree. "See? I told you it would take a silver bullet to get me! Not even a scratch," he added, proudly showing them his arms and legs.

"Don't tell m-me that was just an accident," Gil stammered, running a hand nervously through his hair. "He never even hit the brakes."

"He's right, Rick." Bess seemed quite shaken now. "Maybe there's more than one crazy fan after you."

Nancy bit her lip and thought for a moment. This latest incident confirmed her worst fears. She knew now that the crude attempt on Rick's life on the boat trip was just a sideshow. The main event was still to come.

Gil was still shaking. "Well, I don't know about you folks," he said, "but I've had about all the excitement I can take for one day. Next time we get together, Rick, remind me to take out extra insurance."

"Hey, calm down. It's the price of life in the fast lane, that's all." Rick laughed nervously. "Come on, I'll give you a lift home on my way downtown. Bess?" Turning to Bess, he pulled her gently to him and gave her a lingering kiss.

They walked back to the limo, and Nancy and Gil climbed in. Nancy turned her head away, embarrassed, while Bess and Rick stood on the sidewalk. They were whispering, probably about what had just happened.

Nancy frowned. Things looked bad, very bad indeed. It was as if Bess hadn't even noticed that she and Rick had almost been killed!

"It's just a feeling I get, Ned, but it's a strong one. Something's very wrong here." Nancy flung herself down on the dark blue sofa and filled her boyfriend, Ned Nickerson, in on everything that had happened since she'd arrived in New York. "I only wish you weren't so far away." She sighed wistfully.

"Same here," Ned agreed. "I miss you."

"I miss you, too. And I could really use your help on this case."

"Can I do anything from here?"

"Honestly, I don't think so. Except share a little of your wonderful insight. I'm completely baffled by the whole thing right now."

"Sounds like you need some on-the-scene help. I'd be on the next flight, but I have a big paper due. I do want you to promise not to take any unnecessary chances, though."

"Come on, Ned, you know me. I'm always very careful," Nancy said, teasing him.

"Yes, I know. That's why I want you to keep a low profile. I want you to be in one piece the next time I see you."

Nancy blew a kiss into the phone and said goodbye. After she hung up, she smiled sadly. If only Ned were able to meet her in New York . . .

Just then, the front doorbell rang. Nancy went to open it, and before her stood Mattie Jensen. Her rich auburn hair was pulled up in a ponytail, and she was wearing jeans and a sweatshirt. She looked almost as young as Nancy.

"Hiya, kiddo!" the actress said, bubbling. "Eloise told me she was going to the ballet tonight, so I thought you guys might want a little company."

How could anyone as beautiful and successful as Mattie Jensen be all alone at ten o'clock on a Saturday night? Nancy wondered. It didn't seem possible. But there she was. She's lonely! Nancy realized.

"Sure. Come on in," she said. "Bess is in the shower."

"Hey, I read about what happened to you today on the boat trip. After everything he's been through, Rick must be glad they caught the guy. They said the man tried to throw him overboard."

"Hmm-hmm," Nancy replied, wishing she could have shared Mattie's sense of relief.

"They said the guy was released from a mental institution a few weeks ago."

"I didn't hear that, but from the way he was acting . . ." Nancy's voice trailed off.

"Oh, Nancy, I'm so relieved. Now I'll finally be able to sleep at night!" Mattie smiled softly, but Nancy just turned away. "What's the matter, Nancy? Are you still upset?"

Nancy heaved an enormous sigh. "Mattie, I hate to say this. I know you're not going to like it, but I don't think the man they arrested today is the person we're after."

"But—but they said he'd been stalking Rick for weeks."

"He may have been, but I don't think he's the one who tampered with the light, and sent the chocolates."

Mattie gazed at Nancy in amazement. Then she nodded. "Okay. Tell me why you think it isn't the same person."

"Two reasons. For starters, someone tried to run Rick over tonight."

"No!" Mattie exclaimed.

"I'm afraid so. Don't try to tell Rick that—he insists it was a hit-and-run accident. But I was there, Mattie. The cab never blew its horn, never slowed down—and the license plate was covered over with mud. This all may be circumstantial evidence, but still . . ."

Mattie was silent, taking it all in. "And then," Nancy said, continuing, "there's the photograph of Rick, the one that was all scratched up. It wasn't just a publicity shot, the kind he might autograph for a fan. There was a résumé of all the shows he's been in stapled to the back of it. Correct me if I'm wrong, but actors don't just give out their résumés to the general public, do they?"

"No, of course not. But lots of people would have them."

"Like who? A producer?"

"Sure. When an actor auditions for a job, he always brings a picture and résumé," she said, sitting down. "Pappas would have them. So would the director, and Lillian, of course. His agent would have hundreds. I suppose even Dwayne might have a few left, unless he cleaned out his files recently." Mattie stared at the wall with a faraway look. "But Dwayne is harmless. I'm sure—"

"Wait. Why Dwayne? I thought Rick said he was with International Management."

"Yes, but when Rick was first in New York, Dwayne was his agent. The summer I first met both of them, we were in an acting company doing Shakespeare in Oregon. We were so sure of ourselves," she mused. "Anyway, that fall, we set out for New York and the 'big time.' Rick and I did all right, but Dwayne, who was trying to make it as an actor still, ran into trouble getting parts. He was the wrong type somehow. So, he decided to open a talent agency instead. He really got our careers moving, too."

Just then Bess stepped into the room, a terry bathrobe wrapped around her. "I thought I heard somebody! Hi, Mattie," she chirped. "Did Nancy tell you about our day? Kind of wild, huh?"

"I read about part of it in the paper," Mattie said. "It was—" The telephone rang, interrupting her.

"That's probably for me!" Bess said as she dove for the phone. "Oh, hi!" she purred into the receiver. "Yes, I thought you might— Really? Hmmm—" Suddenly Bess turned a deep crimson and let out a wild giggle. "Umm, just a minute," she said. "I think I'll take this in the other room."

Carefully putting the receiver on its side, Bess gestured wildly at Nancy and then the phone. "It's Rick!" she whispered excitedly. "Hang up for me, okay?" With that, she ran into the bedroom.

Nancy turned to Mattie. She was pale and her glamorous face was drawn tight. Staring vacantly toward the bedroom, her enormous eyes began to fill with tears.

Nancy replaced the receiver. "Mattie . . ." she murmured gently, "you still love him, don't you?"

Mattie collapsed back into her chair. "Yes, I do. Heaven knows why," she answered. "Just a habit, I guess. I've loved him since I first saw him. We've been through a lot together."

Nancy put her hand comfortingly on Mattie's arm. As they listened to Bess giggling happily in the other room, Nancy could feel Mattie's grief. If a girl were talking with Ned like that, she'd be crushed, too.

"But then," Mattie said with a sad smile, "Rick obviously doesn't feel the same way. Well, I'd better go. I might as well get some sleep. We're still having brunch tomorrow morning, right?"

Nancy nodded and walked Mattie to the door, watching as she went down the stairs to her garden apartment. Just as the actress was about to disappear, Nancy remembered what she had been thinking before the phone rang.

"Mattie! Wait!" she called.

The actress looked up from the stairwell. "Yes?"

"How could I get into Dwayne Casper's office? I'd just like to take a look around."

"Well," said Mattie, her brow wrinkling as she thought, "I suppose you could set up an appointment and say you were an aspiring actress. You could even say we did a show together once."

"That might work. I don't think he ever noticed me before. Whenever I saw him I wasn't near you or him. But I don't have any pictures or résumés," she reminded Mattie.

"Oh, that's okay," Mattie assured her. "Just tell him you're new in town. Ask him for advice—he loves that. Dwayne's really good with newcomers, and he'll be flattered that you came to him for guidance. If you call first thing Monday morning and say I told you to call, I guarantee you'll get in. But I promise you, Dwayne is harmless. I should know—we've been friends for years."

"I hope you're right. But if Dwayne's got anything to do with this, I've got to find out. And, Mattie," she said softly, "don't worry about Bess. I know her. She falls in and out of love all the time. She'll get over Rick as soon as she gets back home, you'll see."

Mattie stared into the distance, trying to hide her feelings. "Maybe," she murmured softly. Giving Nancy a strange look, she disappeared down the stairwell to her apartment. Nancy could hear her door close behind her.

That night, tossing and turning in her bed, Nancy couldn't sleep. Her eyes kept popping open, and she'd lie still and stare at the ceiling while her mind was in high gear and she worked through detail after detail. If only they added up.

Rick Arlen. She could picture his handsome face with that winning grin of his, and those sparkling azure eyes. Someone wanted him dead, but who? Rick might not win any popularity contests among the people who knew him best, but only one person hated him enough to want him dead.

It took a very clever person to conceal such powerful hatred so successfully. Nancy tried to imagine who it might be, but there were so many people wishing him ill: Pappas, Casper, Lillian Weiss, and who knows how many others there were just on the set alone. Nancy had had cases this difficult before, and she'd solved them successfully. But this time there were so many possibilities; which one should she investigate first?

As she drifted to sleep, the shadowy figure of Rick came back into her mind. He was signing autographs for a crowd of fans. A monstrous figure walked toward him, slowly stalking him. Nancy tried to cry out, but her voice was caught in her throat. The figure turned toward her, seeing her for the first time. Eyes of indescribable evil glowed at her, paralyzing her with fear.

Then the figure drew a long and sharp knife that glinted in the dim light. Nancy tried to scream, but nothing happened. The shadowy figure was getting closer and closer—

Nancy awoke with a gasp and sat up in bed. The clock-radio by her bed read 5:05 A.M. It was only a dream, thank goodness! she thought, her heart racing. But it was so real.

Sighing with relief, she turned over, ready to

go back to sleep. That's when she noticed that Bess's bed was empty.

In an instant, Nancy was up and out of bed. She hurried into the kitchen—no Bess. She checked the bathroom, the living room, then ran back to the bedroom. Nothing. It couldn't be, but it was.

Bess was gone!

Chapter Ten

THE SOUND OF a car pulling up in front of the building sent Nancy to the window. Opening it and leaning out, she saw a shiny black limousine gleaming in the light of a streetlamp.

A second later Bess stepped out onto the sidewalk. She was followed by Rick, who wrapped his arm around her shoulder. "You won't mind if I don't walk you to the door, will you?" he asked, just loud enough for Nancy to hear.

Bess twirled around and leaned closer into his arms. "Of course not," she said. "I had a great time. It was fun, zipping around the city, just the two of us. Thanks." They fell into a kiss that seemed as if it would never end.

Standing at the window, Nancy was alarmed. As flighty as Bess could be, it wasn't like her to sneak off in the middle of the night. Rick had gone to Bess's head like bubbly champagne. Nancy could only hope her friend wasn't in for a nasty "hangover" when it was all over.

"Nancy!" Bess called out in surprise when she saw her friend waiting for her at the door to the apartment. "What are you doing up?"

"Excuse me," Nancy answered in a low voice, careful not to wake her aunt. "But what are *you* doing up is the question."

Bess's eyes were sparkling. "Oh, Nancy," she said breathily. "New York is so *wonderful!* I've never really noticed before how incredible it is. I just have to live here someday. *Soon.*" Turning to her friend, Bess continued, "We went everywhere. We rode around Wall Street and went to the South Street Seaport and then to this incredible disco, Le Grandine. Absolutely everyone there knew Rick. And he likes me. I mean, he really likes *me!* This could be it! This could be the man I've been looking for all my life!"

"Bess," Nancy began as gently as she could, "didn't you think it might be just a little dangerous to be going out with Rick in the middle of the night when someone is trying to kill him?"

Bess looked annoyed. "Don't spoil this for me, okay?" She walked past Nancy into the apartment and went to their room.

Nancy glared at her friend as she disappeared down the hall. Bess could be so irritating sometimes. Earlier that day she had narrowly missed getting herself killed, and here she was laughing in the face of danger. "You think I'm being silly?" Nancy asked, following after her.

"Of course I do! They arrested the guy, didn't they? Rick convinced me that the runaway cab was only an accident. Besides, nobody would mess with Rick. You should feel his muscles—they're like steel!"

Bess slipped out of her satiny dress and kicked off the slingbacks she had worn to go dancing. Too tired to change into a nightgown, she fell back on the bed in her lacy pink slip.

"Oh, Nancy," she murmured excitedly. "He's so wonderful—and so cute." Reaching over, she snapped off the light between their beds. "Am I going to have happy dreams tonight!"

As Nancy lay in her bed, watching the light of dawn brighten the room, she couldn't help worrying about Bess. This was obviously more than just a schoolgirl crush. And Nancy was more convinced than ever that this fairy-tale romance was not going to have a happy ending.

The clock by Nancy's bed read 9:04 A.M. Bess was still asleep, a contented smile on her lips. Nancy figured she'd be out for a few more hours.

The apartment was quiet. Looking out the window, Nancy saw only one person on the street. The whole city seemed to still be asleep. At eleven, she'd be going out to brunch with her aunt and Mattie, but that was still two hours away.

After pulling on her favorite jeans and slipping her new yellow sweater over her head, Nancy decided that a walk might be just what she needed to help her think and unwind.

Stepping out onto the street, Nancy took a deep breath of the fresh spring air. The birds were singing, and the golden-green leaves on the trees swayed in the morning breeze. On this quiet Sunday morning, with church bells ringing in the distance, New York seemed like a small nineteenth-century town. Nancy loved it. As she walked, she imagined she was part of that older, simpler time.

After a while she came to a tiny park tucked between two buildings. The morning sun was just beginning to warm the benches, and a few people were out with their children, pushing them on swings and watching as they ran and played. Nancy couldn't help herself; she sat down on a bench and let the sun warm her face, relaxing for the first time in days.

A minute later the touch of a hand on her shoulder made Nancy jump. Glancing around, she found herself looking into the dark eyes of Lillian Weiss.

"Well, if it isn't our fair rescuer," Lillian smirked. "Fancy meeting you here."

Nancy was puzzled. New York was a huge city. The odds of running into someone that she knew were small, to say the least.

"Mind if I sit down?" Lillian asked casually. "I'm dead tired. Haven't slept all night."

Nancy moved over to make room for her. She felt uncomfortable in the company of such an unpleasant person, but she didn't want to be impolite.

"Are you still trying to save Rick Arlen's life?" Lillian asked suddenly, looking right into Nancy's eyes.

She certainly is blunt, Nancy thought. Well, I might as well be blunt right back. Whoever was trying to kill Rick already knew that she was on the case. "Still trying," she admitted.

"You really shouldn't bother," Lillian said. She looked down at her feet, so Nancy couldn't read her expression.

"I don't understand," said Nancy, prompting her.

Lillian looked at her curiously, as if she were sizing Nancy up. After what seemed an eternity, she fixed her eyes on Nancy. "Rick is going to die, and there's nothing you can do about it. And I'll tell you something else—whatever happens to him, he has coming. He got where he is by stepping on a lot of people, but he made one mistake. Along the way he stepped on the *wrong* person, and he's going to pay for it."

Nancy couldn't believe what she was hearing. Was this a confession? A warning? She wasn't sure how to take Lillian's statement.

As suddenly as she had appeared, Lillian stood up to leave. "Well," she said, fingering the hem of her purple lamb's-wool sweater, "nice running into you." She gazed at Nancy with a tight smile. "I'll say one thing for you—you've got guts."

Nancy watched as the strange young woman walked away. She was sure now that Lillian had deliberately arranged to run into her. But why? Nancy was more in the dark than ever.

"The restaurant we're going to isn't far away, Nancy. We'll just ring for Mattie on our way out." Eloise was standing in front of the hall mirror, fussing with a teal blue silk scarf. "Is Bess ready yet?"

"Bess!" Nancy called as she knocked on the

door of the room where her friend lay sleeping. "Don't you want to have brunch with us?"

The answer was muffled, so Nancy opened the door. "Leave the address," was all Bess could manage. "I'll meet you there." With that, she flopped over and buried her face in the pillow.

Nancy closed the door. Eloise waited by the main door of the apartment while Nancy wrote down the address and left it on the telephone table. "Ah, youth," Eloise said, smiling wistfully. "I used to be able to sleep like that on weekend mornings. Now I'm always up at the crack of dawn!"

With a wink, Eloise tugged on Nancy's arm. "Shall we? If I wait for my morning coffee much longer, I won't be worth knowing."

As they sat in the restaurant eating eggs Benedict, Nancy couldn't stop thinking of her conversation with Lillian Weiss. The look in her eyes had been so intense. Could it be that Lillian was the one who was trying to kill Rick? Or maybe she was just hiding the identity of the person who really was.

Nancy decided not to mention running into her. Still, she had to know what Lillian's personal situation regarding Rick was. "Mattie," she began offhandedly, "tell me more about Lillian Weiss. I know you said lots of people hate Rick, but she seems to hate him more than most."

Mattie looked up, amazed. "You don't think she's behind it all, do you?"

"I don't really know," Nancy replied. "But I'd like to know more about her."

"Lillian's the one Rick broke up with me for," Mattie blurted out. She looked down at her plate unhappily. "I couldn't believe it when he told me. I mean, I'd stuck by him through all the bad times. When he finally made it, he just dropped me. It was so—" she paused for a moment, unable to go on "—so humiliating." She took out her handkerchief and blew her nose. Suddenly Mattie laughed. "But that's Rick for you. They were only together for two months. He stuck with her till she introduced him to the film people she knew, then he dumped her. I really can't blame Lillian for hating him. I just wish she'd get on with her life. She's just—I don't know —the kind of person who nurses a grudge. The kind that never lets go of anything, know what I mean?"

"Yes," said Nancy thoughtfully. "I think I do."

"Oh, do I dare try one of these?" Eloise was asking with a smile as the waiter held up a plate of miniature pastries.

"Oh, go ahead, Eloise," Mattie said with a

grin, trying to put all thoughts of Rick and Lillian behind her.

Eloise looked at the pastries and thought for a moment. "Why not?" she quipped, lifting a small one onto her plate.

Just then, the manager came up to the table. "Excuse me, ladies. Is there a Nancy Drew at this table?"

"Why, yes," Eloise answered, looking at her niece.

"Ms. Drew, you have a phone call," the manager said. "You can pick it up at the main desk by the coatrack."

"It must be Bess," Eloise guessed. "She probably woke up and realized she'd never be able to make it here after all."

Nancy thanked the manager and made her way to the phone.

"Hi, Bess," she said into the receiver.

But it wasn't Bess. A raspy electronic voice warned her, "Stay away from Rick Arlen, Nancy Drew! And tell your little friend she'd better stay away, too!" With that, the phone line went dead in Nancy's trembling hand.

Chapter Eleven

"BY APPOINTMENT ONLY!" "Put Your Picture And Résumé Under The Door!" "Do Not Ring Buzzer Without An Appointment!"

Nancy read the signs and gulped. Although she'd called earlier and left a message on Dwayne's answering machine, Nancy felt she'd have a better chance of seeing him if she went in person. But getting inside Dwayne Casper's office wasn't exactly going to be easy.

With a sigh and a deep breath, she pressed the buzzer. For a moment it was so quiet that she wondered whether anybody was in the office at all. Then, crisp footsteps sounded on the other side of the door.

"Do you have an appointment?" Dwayne's voice was all business.

"Well, no," Nancy replied. "Not exactly."

"In that case, I suggest you learn to read!"

"But, Mr. Casper!" Nancy said in her most polite voice. "I left a message on your machine. Mattie Jensen said you would talk to me. My name is Diane Elliot. . . ."

Nancy heard a click as he unlocked the door. It swung open, and a smiling Dwayne Casper greeted her. "Well, why didn't you just say you're a friend of Mattie's?" he asked. "Come in! You must understand that if I opened the door to every struggling actor in this town, I'd never be able to get any work done."

"Oh, thank you, Mr. Casper," Nancy said, sounding grateful. In the front reception area was a large empty desk. No receptionist, Nancy noted.

"Right this way," Dwayne said with a sugary smile. He led her into his plush office. "How do you know Mattie?"

"Oh, well, I was an extra on 'Danner's Dream,' and she was kind enough to talk to me. She did say she'd call you about me. But I guess she got busy." That much was true Nancy thought.

Dwayne settled into his chair and looked at her appraisingly. "So you know Luther Parks too?"

"Well, no. Not personally, that is."

"I see. Has Mattie ever seen your work? Apart from extra work, that is."

Here we go, Nancy thought. Time to start lying—and lying big. "Oh, yes," she assured him. "We did a production of *The Sound of Music* together in the Midwest. Mattie played the oldest daughter, and I played one of the younger children."

An amused look passed over Dwayne's face. "That must have been at least eight years ago. Mattie wasn't more than a kid herself back then. Unfortunately, I couldn't see that production."

I know, Nancy thought. That's what Mattie told me.

Dwayne leaned back in his swivel chair. He seemed warm now, even friendly. "So, let me guess, you've come to the big city because you want to be a real actress."

Delighted that the agent had bought her story, Nancy threw herself into her real-life acting role. "Yes, sir," she answered breathlessly.

"Well, well, well— What shall we do about that?" Dwayne pursed his lips, thinking. Then he stood up, walked to the door, and locked it. "So we won't be disturbed," he explained.

A sudden chill made its way down Nancy's spine. If the electronic voice on the phone yesterday had been Dwayne's, she was now trapped.

"What did you say your name was?" Dwayne had a pen poised over a small pink index card.

"Diane Elliot," Nancy said, looking the agent squarely in the eye. "With two *L*s and one *T.*"

"That's a good name for an actress. You're lucky." He smiled. "Now tell me, Diane, why did you come to me? There are hundreds of agents in this city."

"Well, Mattie spoke so highly of you, Mr. Casper," Nancy began. Dwayne's face grew pink with pleasure. "And I know you once represented Rick Arlen—"

At the mention of Rick's name, the agent's face clouded over. "Ah, yes, the irrepressible Mr. A."

"He's not with you anymore, is he?" Nancy was being bolder than she liked to be, but she had to lead Dwayne on.

"Rick? His real name is Richard Aburtuski, by the way. No, he's no longer one of my clients. I don't deal with failures, Ms. Elliot."

Nancy looked genuinely surprised. Dwayne laughed derisively. "You think I'm being ridiculous—after all, he's at the height of success! But I can tell you with certainty that leaving this agency is the biggest mistake Arlen ever made—except for his decision to be an actor, of course. The man can't act his way out of a paper bag. He depends on his looks to get him by, but he'll learn. They all learn eventually that the biggest factor in success is loyalty. And he has none."

Dwayne's face was red with anger. He wasn't through on the subject of Rick Arlen, but just then the buzzer rang. "Whoever it is will go away," he said. "I have no appointments scheduled today."

The buzzer rang through the office once again, and then again and again. Finally Dwayne couldn't stand it anymore. He bolted from his chair and unlocked the door. "I'm going to tell this idiot to go away. Do you have an appointment?" he yelled, hurrying through the reception area. "Because if you don't, you'd better learn to read!"

"But, Mr. Casper! You *must* see me!" Bess's voice was muffled through the door, but her sense of urgency came through loud and clear. "I'm a really great actress and I need an agent! Let me read for you, Mr. Casper, and you can judge for yourself!"

Laughing bitterly, Dwayne called through the door. "Young lady, I'm a very busy man, and I don't handle street performers. Please leave me alone."

"But I'm an *actress!* Just listen." Bess began to recite a passage from *Romeo and Juliet.*

Good old Bess, Nancy thought with a smile. She really was quite an actress when she had to be. They had devised a plan: After Nancy was able to get inside Dwayne's office, Bess would divert his attention so that Nancy could search it. As soon as Dwayne was out of sight in the reception area, Nancy began to rummage through the papers on his desk. The longer Bess was able to divert his attention from Nancy, the more Nancy would be able to find out. And from the sound of things, Nancy thought she just might have all day.

"And I sing, too! Just listen to this, Mr. Casper." Bess launched into a well-known show tune in a loud, off-key voice.

"Please, young woman!" Dwayne begged. "Why don't you go sing in the park or something? You're giving me a headache!"

Aha! Nancy's eyes opened wide as she looked at the papers in front of her. An eviction notice—and several large bills from creditors. Searching further, she found warnings from collection agencies, even threats. Dwayne Casper's talent agency was obviously in desperate trouble.

"But, Mr. Casper, I'm the next Mattie Jensen! Everyone says I look just like her, except I'm prettier."

"What?" Dwayne exploded. *"Nobody,* but *nobody,* ever was, is, or will be prettier than Mattie Jensen! Mattie is one of a kind —absolutely unique!"

Nancy cocked her head to listen. It was clear to her that, where Mattie was concerned, Dwayne's interest was more than just professional.

"Well, I'm unique, too, Mr. Casper—terribly unique and incredibly talented!"

"My dear young woman"—Dwayne was practically screaming now—"if you don't leave at once, I'll call the police. And may I say in parting that with your nerve, you'll probably go far in this business!"

Quickly Nancy put everything back in the desk exactly where she'd found it. When Dwayne returned, he was trying hard to calm down.

"I'm sorry. Now, where were we before that ghastly woman interrupted us?"

Nancy shifted uncomfortably in her seat. Dwayne's eyes had a wild look in them, and having found what she'd come for, all she wanted to do was get out as quickly as she could.

"You know, Mr. Casper, I feel like such a fool, but I just remembered—I've got an appointment with a photographer in fifteen minutes! He's going to take head shots of me."

"Oh, I see," Dwayne replied, still smiling. "Well, is he any good? Maybe I know him. What's his name?"

"His name? Uh—" Nancy panicked for a

moment. What could she say? Finally she blurted out, "Ned Nickerson. He's new in town—just got in from L.A. But Mattie says he's good."

"Hmmm." Dwayne frowned. "Never heard of him. Well, Diane, come and see me when you've got your pictures. I'll see what I can do for you." He extended his hand for her to shake. His grip was firm, like iron, and his eyes searched hers intently.

"Come to think of it, have we met before? You look a bit familiar," Dwayne said.

"Well, we've never actually met," she replied, "but as I said before, I did do extra work on 'Danner's Dream'."

"That must be it, then," he said. "You'd better get going if you don't want to be late for your shoot. Look forward to seeing you again, Ms. Elliot."

"Thank you so much. You've been a great help!" Nancy said and left the office.

Down in the lobby, Bess was munching on a candy bar and smiling broadly. "How'd I do?" she mumbled, her mouth full of chocolate.

"Bravo!" Nancy applauded, laughing. "I especially loved your rendition of 'Tonight.' It was—different, very different."

"You really think so?" asked Bess, fluffing her hair and winking.

"And wait till I tell you what I found!" Nancy said, grabbing her friend by the arm. "But we'd better get over to 'Danner's Dream' right away. I want Mattie to hear this, too."

The crisp spring air whirled around them as they walked briskly up Broadway toward Columbus Avenue.

"He's really in bad shape, huh?" Bess asked incredulously after Nancy filled her in.

"Everybody in the world is after him. And when people are that desperate, it can make them pretty crazy. I want to keep a close eye on Dwayne Casper, Bess. I think he may be our man."

Pushing through the glass doors of Worldwide Broadcasting, Nancy and Bess beamed at the security guard.

"Hi!" Nancy called out. "We're back again."

"Why, hello, girls. You heard the set was closed, didn't you?" the man asked. "They've been having a little trouble in there and Pappas sent down the order. I can't let anybody in, not even you two."

"I know," Nancy told him. "But could you call Mattie Jensen? We just need to talk to her for a few minutes."

The security guard ran his finger down the list of telephone extensions on his desk. "Sure thing. Mattie, let's see— Ah! Here it is."

But before he had a chance to pick up the

intercom, he was interrupted by the boom of a powerful explosion. The sound of shattering glass tore through the air, followed by a blood-curdling scream.

"Nancy!" gasped Bess in terror. "That was Rick!"

Chapter Twelve

WITHOUT WAITING FOR permission, Nancy and Bess followed the security guard backstage. Losing themselves in a mob of people, the girls made their way toward Rick's dressing room.

The lighting designer had been the first to reach the room itself. "Call an ambulance!" he bellowed frantically.

Nancy and Bess arrived a minute later and watched in shock as Kay Wills, the makeup artist, staggered down the hall toward them. Her skin was ashen, and she was trembling all over. Choking back tears, she turned around and sobbed, "It's bad—really bad."

Nancy stood on tiptoe and craned her neck to see inside Rick's dressing room. The first thing that caught her eye was the wide mirror over the makeup table. It had been shattered into a thousand pieces!

An emergency medical team had arrived, and they were on their way up the hall now, pushing aside the crowd of onlookers. "Make room!" Nancy called, flattening herself against the wall.

"Rick! Oh, where is he?" Bess cried frantically. She bit the back of her hand as she strained to get a good look. Just then, Rick appeared in the doorway. He had a stunned look on his face. His blond hair had been blown every which way, and the white towel around his shoulders was stained bright red. Looking down, Nancy gasped—Rick's hands were bleeding!

As soon as the paramedics saw him, they broke into a run. Gathering around him, they picked him up and laid him on a stretcher. They began pulling slivers of glass out of his hands as Rick winced in pain.

"Back off, everybody!" one of the paramedics shouted as the crowd began to press in on them again. In what seemed like just a few seconds, they had finished their immediate task and lifted the stretcher. They carried the wounded star down the hall, out of the building, and into a waiting ambulance.

Once Rick was gone, the bystanders milled around, not knowing what to do. The police arrived and began inspecting the scene, interviewing people, and collecting evidence.

Nancy walked over to Kay, who was now sitting on the floor in a corner of the hall. She still looked pale as a ghost.

"What happened, Kay?" Nancy asked gently, crouching down beside her.

"He was w-wiping off h-his cold cream—" Kay stammered, staring off into space. "And the mirror just exploded! Thank God he had that towel over his face. He'd be blind—worse, maybe. And I was just on my way in there—it could have been me, too!"

A few minutes later, while police combed the area for clues, Pappas assembled the cast and crew.

"Listen up! I have a report from the hospital about Rick." The excited buzzing died down as the producer's voice boomed out into the vast studio.

"He's going to be okay. They said it looked a lot worse than it really was, and that they're going to release him tonight. His hands will be bandaged for a while, of course, but we can work around that. I've already contacted our writers to come up with some material that'll explain his bandaged hands. If we can't work this into the story line somehow, Luther will just stick to closeups. In any case, we're not going to let this shut us down. As far as I'm concerned, you're all still under contract, and that includes Rick. I want everybody back here tomorrow at seven sharp!"

Just then the police officer who had been examining Rick's dressing room let out a long low whistle. "Hey, chief! Look what we found!"

The policeman held up a small metal object. "It's a twenty-four-hour timer. Whoever set this up must have done it yesterday."

Pappas, standing a few feet away, nearly choked. "That's impossible! This set is closed down tight on Sunday. I even hired extra security. My own mother couldn't have gotten in here!"

"Which means," said the chief, "that it was probably an inside job."

Now Nancy finally had a definite lead. She could rule out Dwayne Casper. He couldn't have gotten onto the set to plant the bomb.

But that left her with only two other suspects—Pappas and Lillian. Their faces floated in front of her tightly shut eyes as she leaned against the wall, trying to concentrate amid the confusion.

Nancy shook her head and opened her eyes. She was back at square one with a dangerous killer still on the loose right under her nose!

I've got to get out of here, she suddenly realized.

Quickly, Nancy sprang up and elbowed her way through a group of technicians hovering by the studio door. "Come on," she shouted to Bess. "We've got to go!"

Pulling her friend by the arm, Nancy made straight for the front exit. But she stopped short when she saw Lillian standing directly in front of her, a smug smile on her face. "I'm way ahead of you, Miss Teen Detective," she said, smirking. "Way ahead."

"What's wrong with her?" Bess wanted to know as they hailed a taxi on the corner. "She gives me the creeps."

Nancy didn't answer. She told the cab driver the name of the hospital as they piled in. "And hurry," she added.

Stepping off the elevator on the fifth floor, Nancy and Bess had no trouble finding Rick's room. It was the one with the two police officers in front of it.

Oh, well, thought Nancy, at least he's safe in there. Still, she couldn't help feeling as though she had failed miserably. The police were in on the case now, so there wasn't much point in continuing her investigation. And besides, she hadn't managed to come up with very much, had she?

"Sorry, miss. You can't go in this room,"

one of the officers told Bess when she tried to enter.

"I must see Rick," Bess said frantically.

"A Miss Jensen's in there with Mr. Arlen now."

Bess froze. "Oh. I see—" she finally managed to say. "Has she been there very long?"

"Ever since we got here, miss. About half an hour." He cracked open the door to look inside. "Seems like she might be awhile longer, too."

Bess stepped back, staring anxiously at the half-open door. Through it, she could hear Rick's voice. And it was not the voice of a confident TV star.

"Mattie! Oh, Mattie, I'm so scared. Someone really is trying to kill me!"

"Don't worry, my darling," she replied in a soft voice. "The police are here. They'll protect you."

"You know, Mattie, you were right all along. You were the only one who saw the truth. Mattie, if I come out of this mess alive, I swear I'm going to make everything up to you. I need you, Mattie, I need you so badly—no one else ever meant a thing to me. You're the only one I've ever loved!"

"I've heard enough!" Bess turned and ran down the hall, covering her mouth with her hands.

"Bess! Bess, wait!" Nancy called after her.

"Leave me alone!" She was fighting back her tears but losing the battle. "I can't believe it," she sobbed. "I just can't believe it!"

Nancy started to go after Bess but thought better of it. Right then Bess needed to work this out on her own. But Nancy wondered about the force of her friend's reaction. What was it about this guy that caused women to fall instantly in love with him?

Mattie and Rick had stopped talking, and the police officer silently closed the door again. No sense waiting around, Nancy decided.

Out on the sidewalk, Nancy found Bess. Her eyes were brimming over with tears, and her mascara was smeared all over her face. She looked utterly forlorn.

"Come on, Bess. Let's go home," Nancy suggested, gently taking her friend's hand. Bess nodded listlessly, allowing herself to be led.

The two friends were silent all the way back to Eloise's apartment. Looking over at Bess, Nancy wished she could comfort her somehow. She knew that Bess really hurt. Bess's brave hero had turned out to be not so brave after all. And worse than that, he was in love with someone else.

As they got out of the cab, Nancy caught sight of her aunt Eloise entering the building. "Hi, Aunt Eloise," she called as she hurried up to greet her.

"Hi, Nancy—Bess," she said as they entered the building. "Did you have a nice day?"

"You're never going to believe what happened today," Bess said in a soft voice. She had finally gotten control of herself.

"Well, as soon as we get upstairs, let's kick off our shoes and relax, and you can tell me all about it," Eloise replied, moving toward the mailboxes.

The three were in the mail alcove when Eloise looked down and spotted a small box wrapped in brown paper on the package table. She glanced at it and scooped it up. "Nancy, it's addressed to you," she said, noticing it had no stamps.

As she started to hand it to Nancy, she froze.

The box was ticking!

Chapter Thirteen

NANCY SPRANG INTO action. "Bess, get on the house phone and get someone to call the police."

While Bess was contacting a neighbor, Nancy and Eloise examined the package. "I think the ticking sounds different now," Nancy's aunt said in a frightened whisper. She was still holding the box, but now in trembling hands. "Let's take it outside."

Slowly and calmly, the two went out of the building and walked to the curb. As soon as they had stopped and put the box down, two police bomb-squad officers arrived. It didn't take them long to discover that the box contained an ordinary, harmless alarm clock.

"I've never been so happy to see an alarm clock in my entire life." Nancy's aunt smiled with relief and clasped her hands together to stop them from shaking.

"Somebody went to a lot of trouble to scare your niece, ma'am. And from the sound of this note, that person is serious."

"'Last warning, Nancy Drew, leave town *now,*'" the officer read.

"Nancy, I think maybe we *should* get back to River Heights today." Bess had rejoined them and stood listening as the note was read.

"Bess is right, Nancy. This is serious. Your father would never forgive me if anything happened to you while you were here. Worse, I would never forgive myself. In fact, after the officers leave, I'm calling the airport."

Eloise, Nancy, and Bess thanked the men, and they turned and headed back into the building and up to Eloise's apartment.

Nancy bit her lip. "Wait a minute, Aunt Eloise," she said, trying to stop her aunt from calling the airport. She knew her aunt was only trying to protect her, but how could she leave New York while a dangerous killer was still after Rick? Even if he wasn't the greatest guy in the world, he didn't deserve to die. And obviously, the killer was getting closer and closer. Next time he might succeed.

"Our tickets are for the day after tomorrow," she called out as her aunt was about to lift the phone. "Maybe I can solve the case before then."

"Forget it, Nancy. I'm not going to let you risk your life—not even for a couple more days." Eloise sounded definite. "And besides, the police are on the case now."

"She's probably right, Nancy," Bess agreed.

"Wait a minute, everybody." Nancy was groping for the right words. "You can't ask me to just walk away from this! A man's life is in danger!"

They looked back at her with questioning stares, unconvinced.

"How about this—I promise that if I don't come up with any answers by tomorrow, I'll go straight back to River Heights as we planned originally. But honestly, I could never live with myself if I knew I'd walked away when I could have helped."

Eloise looked down at the floor. Nancy had gotten to her. Bess, despite everything, had to smile. Sleuthing was in Nancy's blood.

"All right, Nancy," Eloise said reluctantly. "I do have only myself to blame—I did introduce you to Mattie."

"Thanks, Aunt Eloise," Nancy cried warmly, throwing her arms around the older woman's shoulders. "You're a peach, you know that?"

"Some peach. I invite you to New York for a vacation, and you wind up running all over town, tracking down a murderer. And getting bomb threats delivered to your door!"

"He or she is *not* a murderer—not yet, anyway," Nancy said. "Nobody's been killed, and I hope we can keep it that way. Now, if you'll excuse me, there's something I've got to take care of right away."

"Who's there?" came Mattie's surprised voice in response to Nancy's knock.

"It's me. May I come in?"

"Oh, Nancy," Mattie said when she opened the door. "Wasn't it awful?" Mattie looked exhausted. Obviously, she had just been through quite an ordeal. "Come on in," she added distractedly. "Sorry the place is such a mess. I just got back from the hospital."

"How's Rick doing?" Nancy asked.

"He's going to be okay. But—oh, Nancy, his hands! They hurt him terribly. I just can't believe he's actually going to do the show tomorrow."

"What?" she gasped. "Tomorrow?"

Nancy was truly amazed—he had sounded so frightened at the hospital. I have to give him a lot of credit, she thought. He really was brave.

"Pappas showed up at the hospital. He just burst in past the guards. I was there for the whole thing. He couldn't stop apologizing for this and all the other things that have been happening on the set lately. He even promised to hire Rick a bodyguard and to get some plainclothes detectives to be at the studio until this whole thing is over. But Rick said something about loyalty to his fellow actors, and just shrugged it off and told Pappas he'd be back at work tomorrow. As shaken up as Rick was, he just couldn't say no." She sighed miserably.

"I don't know how I'm going to get through tomorrow," she said. "I'm so worried about him. Oh, Nancy, what am I going to do? If he's killed, I'll just—I'll—oh, I don't know what I'll do!" Mattie seemed to be on the brink of hysteria.

"Hold on, Mattie. It's going to be okay," said Nancy, trying to comfort her. "I'm still here, and I've got one more day in town. I haven't given up yet."

Mattie looked into Nancy's eyes, and a glimmer of hope showed on her face. "You—you mean it?"

"Mmm-hmm. Maybe I'm not exactly closer to solving this case, but I sure know a lot more than when I started. And I'll do my best for you until it's time for me to leave," Nancy assured her. "Please don't worry."

But what Nancy didn't tell Mattie was that

she was hoping the criminal would try again and this time make a mistake—the kind of mistake he or she had managed to avoid until then. Her experience showed that most criminals tripped themselves up sooner or later.

"Oh, I hope you're right," Mattie said with a nervous laugh. "I guess I'd better get you and Bess hired on as extras again, huh?"

When it was all arranged, Mattie went back to the hospital to get Rick, and Nancy went back upstairs for a quiet dinner with her aunt and Bess.

Just before turning in, she went into the empty living room, picked up the phone, and dialed. She was in luck.

"Twice in one week?" came Ned's familiar voice. "What's going on, Nancy? Could this be true love?"

Nancy giggled, with a wave of warm feeling passing over her. Good old Ned. He was just what she needed right then—the voice of sanity. "You know I love you," she said with a laugh. "But thanks for trying to be funny. I can use a little humor right now."

"Things aren't going too well there, are they?"

"That's putting it mildly," she said, and told him the latest developments in the case.

Ned tried to sound comforting. "Look, Nancy, I've known you for a long time, right?"

"Forever," she replied.

"And in all that time, I've never seen you blow a case. So just hang in there. You'll figure it out."

"But, Ned, I have only one more day!" she protested.

"Something will happen, and the pieces will all fall into place. You'll solve this one, I know you will, Detective Drew."

"Well, I'm glad somebody thinks so." She sighed, not really convinced. "I appreciate the vote of confidence, though."

"And, Nancy . . ."

"Yes, Ned?"

"Be careful, okay? I'd hate to have anything happen to you."

Once again, the girls were slated to play nurses. Rick's injuries had been written into the script. In the *new* story line, Rory, in a fit of despair, would try to throw himself out a window. He would be rescued, but not before he had cut his hands to pieces and had to be taken to the hospital.

"Nancy! How do I look?" Bess asked later that day. Twirling around in her nurse's uniform, she fluffed her red wig carefully so the pert white nurse's cap wouldn't fall off. Her heart didn't seem half as badly broken since she had found out she'd be working on "Danner's Dream" again that day. She even had a "silent bit"—she was the nurse who would greet Serena when she arrived at the hospital.

"I called my mother to make sure she'd tape the program," Bess said excitedly. "Then I can take it around to casting directors and stuff."

Nancy smiled at her friend. Even in the middle of all this craziness, she was still managing to have a good time. Of course, her fun was tempered by her feelings for Rick. Whenever she saw him on the set, she turned and purposely avoided him.

"Oh, and you know what? I found out that that lady with glasses and clipboard over there is the casting director," Bess whispered, pulling Nancy by the arm. "I'm going to go hang around her for a while. You never can tell, Nancy, this could be *it.* And won't Rick feel like a fool when I become a bigger star than he ever was!"

Nancy sighed and looked at her friend. "Bess, as a friend, I've got to tell you this: You are totally insane!" Then pushing her friend playfully, she whispered, "But go for it. I hope she notices you. I'll see you when it's time for our scene, okay? I want to check out Rick's new dressing room."

Rick was dressing and being made up in an improvised area across the hall from the costume room. He sat staring listlessly into space, still stunned by what had happened the day before. Kay was with him.

"So, Rick," she was saying, trying to cheer him up, "are you going to give me a hand here, or do I have to do this all myself?"

But Rick didn't move. He seemed so scared —as though there was a voice inside his head telling him over and over again that someone was trying to kill him. And that he or she might very well succeed.

Nancy leaned up against a wall and watched as Kay put some warm water into the sink. "No mirrors in here, I hope you've noticed," she said, trying to make a joke. When she saw she wasn't getting through to Rick even a little bit, she sighed wearily and picked up a stick of makeup.

"Okay, here we go," she said, uncapping it. Then, "Oops!" she cried as the stick slipped out of her hands and fell into the wet sink.

"Clumsy me," she said to herself, shaking her head. Suddenly, there was a hissing noise. The water in the sink began bubbling furiously.

"What the—?" Rick gasped. A sharp odor rose from the sink.

Nancy recognized the smell. "That's acid," she whispered.

"Oh, my God!" Kay cried, her hands on her cheeks as she watched the acid eat holes in the stainless steel sink. "Rick, that could have been your face!"

Chapter Fourteen

"THAT'S IT!" RICK exclaimed, "I've had it!" He tried to pick up his suede jacket, but even a simple action such as this was difficult because of the bandages on his hands. Growling with disgust, he stormed out of the room.

"Rick?" Kay called, following him down the corridor. "Where are you going?"

"Forget it, Kay. I'm taking a nice long walk and going someplace where nobody can find me."

Just at that moment, a beet-faced William Pappas stepped into the hallway. "What's going on here?" he asked as the handsome actor flew down the hall.

"I'm out of here. Off the show. I'm not taking any more chances."

"But you're under contract, Arlen! You can't just leave!"

"Oh, yeah? Watch me." With that, Rick pushed past the angry producer and made his way toward the entrance.

Pappas made a lunge for him, but a couple of crew members restrained him.

"Come on, Mr. Pappas, calm down," they urged him. "Give him a break. The guy's been under a lot of stress lately."

Pappas let the men straighten his suit as he muttered under his breath, "He's under tension? What am I—chopped liver? I'm behind schedule, and the network is breathing down my back. I have ratings to think of!"

But it was too late. Rick was out the door and gone. Nancy and Kay looked on as the producer fumed, powerless to stop him.

Seconds later Luther Parks hurried up to them, running a hand nervously through his silver hair. "Bill, someone just said Rick Arlen left! What do you want me to do?"

But Pappas was in no mood for creative solutions. "You're the director," he snarled, heading back to his office. "Think of something!"

Luther shrugged and turned to Lillian, who was standing beside him. "We'll shoot the hospital scene with Mattie," he said.

"Whatever you say," Lillian drawled, throwing a wink Nancy's way. "Report to duty, Nurse Drew. And try not to miss your cue."

Standing in the make-believe operating room as the crew adjusted the lights, Nancy's spirits sank. Rick was out on the street somewhere, unprotected. And there she was on her last day in town, about to walk around in the background of a fictional scene instead of tracking down a very real criminal.

Someone had found a way to get around the set undetected, again and again. That was the key. In spite of guards at the doors, and people everywhere, Rick's enemy had gotten in. If she only knew how! If she could only discover the method behind the madness, she felt sure the rest would fall into place. But how could she do anything now?

"Action!" came Lillian's voice. Taking her medicine tray, Nancy crossed the set, put the tray down, and walked back again, heaving a deep sigh.

Action. That's exactly what was needed. If only there was some action she could take!

"Cheer up, Nancy." Bess peered sympathetically into the mirror at her friend's reflection. Nancy wasn't used to losing and it hurt. Bess pulled a comb through her blond hair and twisted it up in one deft move. She fastened it in place, and searched for something comforting to say. "I know it's a bummer, but you win some and you lose some." Somehow those weren't the words she had been looking for.

"Well, I don't really feel like going out to dinner, that's for sure," Nancy replied listlessly. She reached for her makeup case on the bathroom counter.

"But we're going to a really great restaurant! Your aunt, Eloise, said it's one of her favorites. And I can't wait to tell her about my big scene today. The videotape editor told me he was sure I got into the shot. Can you imagine? There I am, actually handing a paper to Mattie Jensen on national TV! My mother will flip!"

Nancy lifted the collar of her mauve jacket and fastened a rhinestone pin to the lapel. "There's just so little time left and so many unanswered questions."

Suddenly the door buzzer rang. "Come on, Nancy. That's the signal. Your aunt and the cab are waiting!" Bess cried. "Be right down!" she called into the intercom.

At the restaurant the girls were seated by a lovely young hostess, who looked more like a model than a restaurant employee.

"Pierre will be your waiter," she told them.

Just then, a young man with twinkling eyes and a handlebar mustache approached the table.

"Bonsoir. Je m'appelle Pierre. Here I haf ze menu," he said in a thick French accent. Bess couldn't help giggling as he handed the menus around the table, giving each of them a seductive look. "I can tell zees table will be my favorite of ze night."

"I didn't know this place served French food," Eloise mused out loud, watching him go.

"It doesn't," Bess remarked in surprise as she looked over the menu. "A French waiter at an American restaurant. That's weird."

"Not for New York it's not," Nancy's aunt replied.

Nancy's eyes followed the waiter to the bar, where he put in an order for some other customers. "Hey, Steve," he yelled in a regular voice, "give me three mineral waters and a Coke."

Nancy looked up when the waiter returned to the table to take their order. *"Garçon—avez vous un stylo noir, peut-être?"*

"Huh?" he asked, confused. "Want to run that by me again, lady?"

"You're *not* French?" Bess exclaimed.

"Mais non, mademoiselle," the waiter admitted with a shy smile. "I mean, nope. Never even seen the place."

"I'll bet I know what's going on," Eloise ventured. "You're an actor, aren't you?"

The waiter looked at Eloise for a second and then laughed. "Okay, okay. I confess. I'm guilty. I am an actor, but please don't be mad."

With that, he tugged on the end of his mustache and pulled it off. "I have an audition for the part of a French waiter tomorrow, so I thought I'd get in a little practice tonight. Now, ladies, what can I get you?" He proceeded to take their orders and then left.

"Does that happen a lot around here?" Bess asked.

Eloise smiled and shook her head no. "But many of the waiters in New York are actors, Bess. And a lot of the delivery people, word processors, dog walkers . . . They do many different kinds of work just to survive between acting jobs."

Bess was sobered by the thought that an acting career could be so difficult. But Eloise's words also had a great impact on Nancy.

"Playing different roles," she murmured softly to herself. Suddenly a big piece of the puzzle had fallen into place. That's how the culprit does it, she told herself. Hadn't she herself gone anywhere on the set completely unnoticed in her nurse's uniform? No one had even looked at her twice. Of course! How could she have missed it?

"And when the director called 'action' I was supposed to be sorting these papers at the front desk," Bess was telling Eloise. "And Mattie walks right up to me and says, 'Excuse me. Did Rory Danner leave a message for me?' And I nod and I hand her an envelope. We must have done the scene six times, right, Nancy?" Bess didn't wait for an answer. She just went on, filling Eloise in on every little detail of her big day on "Danner's Dream." Nancy ate her dinner in silence, trying to put the final pieces of the puzzle together.

"I'm stuffed," Bess said as they climbed the stairs to Nancy's aunt's apartment. "That dessert was too much."

"After you girls leave, I'm going to have to go on a diet," Eloise said, reaching into her bag for the keys.

Just then, through the door they heard the phone ring. "Don't worry—the machine will get it," Eloise said, letting them in and flicking the lights on.

"Hello," came Eloise's recorded voice on the answering machine. "I can't come to the phone right now, but if you leave a message at the sound of the beep, I'll get back to you as soon as I can."

"This message is for Nancy Drew." A shiver

ran down Nancy's spine. It was the voice of Lillian Weiss. "It's Lillian, Nancy. There's something I have to tell you. It's a matter of life and death. Meet me on the set tomorrow morning at six o'clock, before rehearsal. I'll leave a pass for you."

Chapter Fifteen

"NANCY, YOU'RE NOT thinking of going, are you?" The color drained from Eloise's face, and she sat down on the sofa. "You told me yourself that you thought this woman might be the killer. I can't allow you to put your life in danger that way, even to save someone else's. You're my niece, and you're the only child my brother has. Think how he would feel if something happened to you!"

Nancy sat down beside her aunt and took her hand. "Aunt Eloise," she said calmly, "ever since I was a little girl, I've been trying to solve mysteries. I can't quit now! It's my life, Aunt Eloise. It's what I do best. Don't ask me to give it up now, please."

Tears in her eyes, Eloise hugged her niece fiercely. "I'll be biting my nails the whole time, you know that?" she said with a resigned laugh. "But why do you have to meet at the studio?"

"Oh, you know how dramatic soap people are. Just a little added mystery. Now, come on, there's nothing to worry about," Nancy countered with a smile. "And besides, I know quite a lot of karate, remember? All those lessons ought to be good for something."

When she got to Worldwide Broadcasting, Nancy picked up her pass at the security desk, then slipped into the main corridor. Every muscle in her body was tensed. There was something wrong about all this—she knew it the moment she had heard Lillian's voice. But something drove her on, step by step, toward the studio.

As she turned down a corridor, she saw someone and ducked back around the corner. It was the janitor, mopping the floors. Not wanting to run into anyone, she went back around, taking the long way to the studio in order to avoid him.

Finally, she reached the vacuum-sealed door and pushed her way in. The set was dimly lit, but Nancy's eyes adjusted to the darkness. At first it seemed to be deserted, but then Nancy saw her.

Lillian was sitting on a chair on the set of the Danner kitchen, holding her head in her hands. As Nancy approached, she turned around.

"Our fair rescuer," she said under her breath. "How kind of you to come." The words were full of bravado, but the old self-assured Lillian was gone. The mocking look had disappeared, and Lillian's face was now fearful.

"Why did you ask me to come here?" Nancy demanded. "What's all this about?"

"Oh, I'm not the maniac, if that's what you're worried about. In fact, I asked you here because—" Lillian's voice wavered. "Because he's after *me* now."

Nancy crossed the room and sat down next to Lillian. Then she listened intently to every word of her story.

"When things started turning weird around here, I got curious. Actually, I was kind of hoping Rick would get what he deserved, if you get my meaning. But then I found something. It was that day I ran into you in the hall. I had just found it in a closet. I didn't want to tell anyone about it, so I hid it where no one would come across it."

"The prop room, of course!" Nancy's eyes

lit up. So that was why Lillian had acted so secretively that day!

"Right. And this little item I found made me want to find out more. So I did. I kept on finding more and more, until—" Lillian's voice was barely a whisper. "Until I got this yesterday." She handed Nancy a typewritten note. "Were you thinking of blackmail, my pet?" it read. "Not if I kill you first."

"So you see," Lillian went on, "that's why I called you here. In case anything happens to me. I mean, I knew you were on the case, and, well, you understand." She picked up a shopping bag that lay at her feet and, taking something out of it, she held it up for Nancy to look at.

"A long-haired wig, glasses, a T-shirt—" Nancy sifted through the contents, her suspicions confirmed. "It looks like a disguise. Whoever it was used it to get around the set unnoticed."

"Exactly," Lillian agreed. "And what better disguise than as a stagehand? One of those anonymous people walking around during every shoot. Everyone else is so busy doing their work, no one notices. It's perfect!"

"What else did you find?" Nancy asked.

"Oh, more of the same. Different every day. I knew immediately that it was an actor. Or an ex-actor—"

Then I was right! Nancy said to herself.

"You see," Lillian went on, "I finally put two and two together. Which, I hate to say, is more than you've done."

"I take it you have proof of the maniac's identity, then," Nancy said.

"Of course I do," she said with a wicked smile. "It is—"

Lillian didn't get a chance to finish her sentence. All of a sudden, every light in the entire studio flashed on. Shading her eyes, Nancy glanced up to the director's booth, where the lighting controls were.

There, looking down at them from behind the thick Plexiglas, was Dwayne Casper! His expression was furious, and in his hand was a gun—pointed straight at Nancy!

Chapter Sixteen

"WELL, HELLO, YOU two!" Dwayne's voice boomed at them, seeming to come from every imaginable direction. He let out a monstrous laugh. "I only followed Lillian, but I've trapped both of you. How lucky! Congratulations, your death scenes will look so lovely on videotape. A videotape for my personal viewing pleasure only!"

For an instant, Dwayne relaxed his grip on the gun a bit. Nancy, seeing her chance, made a dash for the door. Just as she reached it, she heard it go *whoooossshh,* and the red light above it flashed on. The door was locked—vacuum sealed.

"Are we locked up down there?" Dwayne screamed in a grotesque parody of Luther Parks. He laughed again. "A little stage fright, Ms. Elliot? Actually, I didn't know until yesterday that you and Ms. Elliot were one and the same. Very good bit of acting. Very realistic. You see, we strive for realism here—real bullets, real blood, real death." He waved his gun playfully at them.

"You two are only the first act. Rick Arlen's death will be the climax of my little soap opera. He's gotten away from me so far, thanks to you, Nancy Drew. But with you two little nuisances out of the way, I don't think he has much of a chance. Do you?"

Dwayne paused, waiting for a reply. Nancy had to think fast. This might be her only chance to save her life and Lillian's. Somehow she had to distract him, make him forget he had a gun.

"Dwayne, why? Why do you hate Rick so much? Lillian and Mattie have more reason to hate him than you do!"

Her words seemed to ignite Dwayne's fury. He exploded at her, just as he had at Bess that day in his office.

"More reason than I? What do you know about it? Keep your ignorant little mouth shut! Rick Arlen has to die, and I'll tell you why. Because he killed me, that's why. He killed Dwayne Casper."

Dwayne paused for breath. Nancy had the feeling Dwayne's story was a long one. That was good. She needed time—time to think of a way out.

"I was an actor," Dwayne cried, all the hurt and rage in him pouring out with his story. "I'd studied every aspect of my craft and was a master of Shakespeare, dialects, stage combat—everything. I was underrated and underappreciated—but brilliant. Then I met Mattie.

"We fell in love, and I was the happiest man on earth. Then—then came August. We did *Romeo and Juliet.* Mattie was Juliet, but Rick beat me out for the role of Romeo. The director was a sucker for a pretty face, and so, I soon found out, was Mattie.

"From that moment on, my life was never the same. And I never forgot what he had done to me."

As Dwayne ranted on, Nancy looked around desperately for some way out.

"I am not like some people, who fall in love every day," he rasped. "When I lost Mattie, I knew that I would never love anyone ever again. I decided that if I couldn't have her, I'd make money, lots of money. I gave up acting and became an agent instead.

"I made them stars. I did it all. And how did Rick pay me back? By leaving me, that's how. I got nothing in return for all my hard work—nothing at all. He had destroyed me again.

"Once Rick left, other clients began to leave. All I had left was Mattie. And then—" Dwayne paused, and his expression grew dark with rage. "Then he started luring Mattie away from me. That's when I decided to kill him. Which brings me back—" he raised the gun at Nancy, looking down at them "—to you two ladies."

"Dwayne!" Nancy shouted, shaking him out of his daze. "Your story sounds like a soap opera. That stuff doesn't happen in real life!"

"That shows what you know about life, Nancy Drew," Dwayne rasped into the mike. "Real life *is* a soap opera. You'll learn that. Or rather, you would have, had you lived."

"Rick didn't kill you," Nancy insisted. "You're still—"

Dwayne erupted again. "Enough!" he screamed. "It's time for the final closeup. I'm going to write you two out of the script forever."

Quickly, he disappeared from sight. Nancy guessed that he was on his way down to the set. That only gave her a few seconds to think of something.

Nancy looked frantically around. Lillian was standing, shocked, unable to help in any way. She was frozen with fear. As clever as she had been in figuring out who the criminal was, she was utterly useless right then.

In the few seconds she had left, Nancy scanned the set, looking for something —anything. Then, she saw it.

Over in the corner stood a large metal cylinder. On it were written the words "Smoke Machine." Rushing over to it, Nancy found the control switch and turned it to the Dense setting.

Not a moment too soon, either. Seemingly from nowhere, Dwayne appeared.

"Ah, there you are, my nosy little friend. Would you care to rejoin Ms. Weiss onstage?"

Nancy moved slowly back to the kitchen area, hoping that her plan would work.

"What's that hissing?" Dwayne turned and looked around nervously, but all he could see was the nearer half of the studio. The rest was hidden by a thick white fog, which was made even worse by the spotlights.

Quickly, while his back was turned, Nancy grabbed Lillian by the arm and pulled her into the protection of the fog. By the time Dwayne realized what was happening and turned around again, they were gone!

Dwayne cursed loudly as Nancy dragged Lillian into a foggy corner on the set. She left Lillian there and began to walk toward the sound of Dwayne's voice. She had to get the jump on him from behind.

Then she heard a sound that made her heart sink. It was the sound of a giant fan—the wind machine.

"Very clever, Nancy Drew," came Dwayne's voice through the diminishing fog. "But there's an antidote for every poison, or vice versa."

The fog was now down to a very small area, and Nancy knew that her time was running out. Crouching down, she took a deep breath and prepared to make a desperate dive at Dwayne. He would still have the gun, she knew. She had only one advantage—surprise.

Rearing back, Nancy flung herself through the air at Dwayne. At the last moment, he turned and saw her. The two of them fell together, toppling over each other, and Dwayne's gun emptied itself.

Chapter Seventeen

THOSE WERE GUNSHOTS coming from the set!"

"Quick, this way!"

When the police raced onto the set they found Dwayne Casper flat on the floor. On top of him was Nancy Drew, holding his arms in a double hammerlock.

"His gun is on the floor over there," she told the police breathlessly as they relieved her of her burden.

"Nancy!" Eloise exclaimed, rushing over to her.

"I'm fine, really, Aunt Eloise."

"Well, all the karate lessons in the world

wouldn't have helped if this bullet had come any closer!" Eloise poked at the sleeve of Nancy's jacket. In it was a charred round hole the size of a dime.

Nancy looked down at the hole, her heart skipping a beat. "Please, don't tell Dad," she begged. "And I promise I'll be more careful from now on."

Throwing her arms around her niece, Eloise sighed. "Oh, Nancy, I'm just glad you're alive!"

Bess rushed up to them and threw her arms over theirs in a three-way hug. "Thank goodness, you're all right!" she cried. "When we heard the shots—" She couldn't go on.

The police had handcuffed Dwayne, who stood there passively, a dull look in his eye.

"Do you know how close I was to paying Arlen back for all he's done to me?" he began telling the police officer, who stood impassively beside him clutching his arm. "Do you know how long I worked to get this close?" Dwayne muttered bitterly, his hands locked behind his back.

"Tell your story to the sergeant, buddy," the police officer said. "Ms. Drew, I'll need to get a statement from you and from Ms. Weiss. Would you see that she makes it down to the station house?"

"Of course," Nancy agreed. In all the commotion, she hadn't even given a thought to Lillian. Apparently, the fright had been a bit too much for her—she'd fainted.

"I *had* to call the police, Nancy," Eloise was explaining. "Something told me you weren't safe, and I had to."

At the door, Dwayne spun around suddenly. "Rick Arlen was going to die. He should have died! And I would have killed him if it hadn't been for you, Nancy Drew!"

"Whew." Bess sighed as the officer pushed Dwayne outside. "He's crazy—"

"He's in the right hands now," Nancy added soberly. "And not a moment too soon, either."

"Flight four-seventeen will be boarding at gate three in five minutes."

"That's our flight, Aunt Eloise," said Nancy, putting down her luggage so she could give her aunt a hug.

"You must promise me you'll come again soon—maybe in the fall?" Eloise asked. "And give your father my love, will you? Goodbye, Bess—I hope I'll see you again soon."

But when Nancy and Bess turned to go, they heard their names being called out.

"Nancy! Bess, wait!" A familiar voice floated down the airport corridor. Turning around, Nancy saw a radiant Mattie Jensen running toward them, her auburn curls flying around her face. "We couldn't let you leave without saying goodbye," she cried.

Beside her, Rick Arlen was cradling two large bouquets of roses in his arms. He handed the first to Nancy and said, "Thank you for saving my life, Nancy—I don't know what I would have done without you."

Then he turned to Bess, who seemed more than a little flustered. "This one is for you, love," he murmured, giving her the flowers.

"Oh, Rick, thank you," she cried, letting down her guard. For a minute, Nancy almost felt sorry that she had been thinking of him as such a heel. She was sure the flowers were his way of saying he was sorry for toying with Bess's emotions.

But the hopeful light went out of her eyes when he explained, "They're from Pappas. He asked us to give them to you."

"Pappas sent us flowers?" asked Nancy incredulously.

"Oh, he's really a teddy bear," said Mattie. "And he's on top of the world now that the show's back on track."

"He even agreed to cancel my contract with no hard feelings," Rick said, laughing. "In fact, he's already written it into the script. I'm getting killed next week, and I go to work on my feature the week after. Ironic, isn't it? Rick Arlen lives, but Rory Danner bites the dust!"

"And Pappas rehired everyone that he

fired," Mattie added. "All thanks to you, Nancy."

Nancy's eyes twinkled. Nothing beat the wonderful feeling she always had after solving a case. "I'm glad I could be of some help," was all she could say.

"But the best news of all is—" Rick flashed Mattie a million-dollar smile. "Shall I tell them, or do you want to?"

Mattie beamed. "You go ahead."

"Mattie has agreed to marry me," he announced proudly. "We're flying to her parents' house next weekend. All this made me realize that there's only one woman in the world for me." He looked somber for a moment, adding, "Thank goodness it wasn't too late."

Nancy noticed that Rick avoided Bess's eyes as he spoke. "Well," Nancy said, "that's great news, you two. Congratulations." Looking over at her friend, Nancy could tell that Bess wished she were in Mattie's shoes. "Well, we'd better get going, though," Nancy said. "See you next time we're in New York!"

With that, and a final squeeze of her aunt's hand, Nancy put her arm around Bess's shoulders and walked past the Passengers Only sign.

"I'm sorry it worked out like this, Bess," she told her friend. News like that had to hurt.

"Oh, it's okay," Bess said and sighed. "I'm just so tired."

Nancy adjusted the strap of her carry-on bag

with a weary smile. "I know what you mean. After a vacation like this, we really need a vacation!"

"So tell me," said George, leaning forward over a hot fudge sundae and crinkling her nose. "Is Rick Arlen really as gorgeous in real life as he is on TV?"

Nancy looked over at Bess, wondering how she would respond.

"Not nearly," Bess replied. "He's kind of short, and those fabulous blue eyes are really contacts."

Nancy rolled her eyes. Bess was laying it on just a little thick.

"And you actually had a date with him?" George was practically shouting. Bess just turned her face away. "I can't believe it!" George went on. "I'm so jealous! What was he like? What did you do?"

"Uh, George—she doesn't want to talk about it," Nancy warned, finally able to interrupt.

"Oh, I get it." George nodded. "Well, you did get to be on television—and on 'Danner's Dream,' " she exclaimed cheerfully.

"Yeah—" Bess sighed. "But seeing how actors and actresses really live, and how hard they work, I don't know. I've been thinking of becoming a model instead." With that, she took an enormous mouthful of strawberry ice cream.

"Oh, really?" Nancy said skeptically. "Will you go on your famous ice cream diet?"

"She's got to look her sundae best," quipped George in reply.

Bess, however, was not amused. "Lay off, you two, will you?" she said testily. "I'm depressed enough as it is."

"Sorry, Bess," said Nancy. "There'll be other guys."

"Not for me," Bess insisted, shaking her head vehemently. "I'm through with men forever." She put down her spoon and gazed out the window dejectedly.

Suddenly her attention was caught by someone passing in front of the window—someone tall, male, and very good-looking. "Hey, who is *that?*" she asked eagerly. "He must be new in town. I never would have missed someone like that."

But neither George nor Nancy could answer. Both of them were doubled up with laughter.

Same old Bess!

THE NANCY DREW FILES™

Case 18

Circle of Evil

Carolyn Keene

Chapter One

WITH A SMILE, Ned Nickerson leaned toward Nancy Drew and put his lips close to her ear. "I thought this was supposed to be a small party," he said loudly. "So far, I've counted thirty people, and another twelve are just walking in the door."

Laughing, Nancy raised her voice so Ned could hear her over the pounding rock music. "Maybe this is small to Joanna," she shouted. "After all, forty-two people barely fill one wing of this house."

It was true. Joanna Tate's home was such a

huge, sprawling place that people jokingly called it the River Heights Hotel. The Tates were rich, and they loved to spend money —on their house, their cars, jewelry, antiques, and especially travel. That was the funny thing about them, Nancy thought. They had a fantastic house filled with just about everything money could buy, and they hardly spent any time in it. The three of them had barely arrived home from a month-long trip to Europe when Mr. and Mrs. Tate repacked their bags to catch another plane, this time to Mexico. When Joanna had invited Nancy to the party, she said she was tired of being on the move and wanted to spend a few weeks just lounging by the pool of the River Heights Country Club.

The club was where Nancy and Joanna had met. Nancy's father, lawyer Carson Drew, belonged to it, and so did the Tates. As a detective, Nancy was usually too busy working on cases to spend any time there, but one of the few times she had been there she struck up a conversation with Joanna.

Actually, Joanna was the one who had started the conversation. She loved to talk, Nancy discovered, especially about things she had just bought or was about to buy. Nancy had never known anyone more into *things* than Joanna, and if it weren't for her great sense of humor, her conversation would be boring after a while. In fact, the two of them didn't have much in common except that they were both eighteen and they were both girls. But they had become friendly in spite of their lack of common ground, and Joanna had invited Nancy to her next big bash. Nancy had just finished a case and was definitely in the mood for a party.

"This band is great," she said to Ned, looking around the terrace where the five-piece band was playing. It was a warm summer night, and a lot of people had come outside to dance. "I should have known Joanna wouldn't just pop a cassette into a tape deck. Trust her to hire a live band." Tossing her reddish blond hair back from her face, she stood up and took Ned's hand. "Come on, let's dance!"

The two of them found space on the crowded terrace and danced five songs, until the band took a break. Then they went inside and made their way to the refreshment table, where there was enough food to feed a small village for a year. Nancy was trying to decide between a piece of the twelve-foot-long hero or a slice of pepperoni pizza when Bess Marvin and Bess's cousin, George Fayne, Nancy's two best friends, joined her and Ned.

"Isn't this incredible?" Bess shook her long blond hair and laughed as she piled food on her plate. "I guess I'll have to start my diet tomorrow."

George, who was tall and slim and never had to watch her weight, laughed, too. "I keep telling you that you don't need to go on a diet. All you need is more exercise."

"I do exercise," Bess protested. "I just danced for half an hour, thanks to that fabulous band. I never knew what you saw in Joanna," she said to Nancy, "but I have to admit, she does know how to throw a great party."

"Where is Joanna, anyway?" Ned asked. "I haven't seen her since we got here."

"Probably trying on another outfit she bought in Europe," George commented.

"There she is," Nancy said, and they all turned as Joanna Tate, a short girl with frizzy brown hair and a wide smile, burst into the room. As George had said, she was wearing an outfit that couldn't have been bought at a River Heights shopping mall, but her clothes didn't stand out as much as her voice. As usual, Joanna was talking a mile a minute.

"Nancy!" she cried, edging her way over to the food table. "Hi! Glad you all could make it."

"It's great to be here," said Nancy.

"The band is excellent!" Bess exclaimed. "And your dress is gorgeous."

Joanna twirled around so that Nancy, Bess, George, and Ned could get the full benefit of her electric blue silk dress, which was embroidered with hundreds of tiny pearls. When she finished modeling, she asked, "Oh, Nancy, did I tell you about my new necklace yet?"

"Necklace?" Nancy shook her head. "I don't think so."

"Well, actually, I'm not supposed to mention it, but it's so fabulous that I just can't keep it a secret a minute longer!" her voice lowering a bit.

"Why should you have to keep a necklace secret?" George asked.

"Because," Joanna explained, "it's very rare and very valuable. It once belonged to a Russian countess, and my daddy paid a small fortune for it. He promised to give it to me when I'm twenty-one." She rolled her eyes and giggled. "If he knew I was even talking about it, he'd cancel my credit cards!"

"That must be some necklace," Ned remarked.

"It is," Joanna agreed. "It's absolutely gorgeous. I wish you could see it. It's got diamonds and rubies as big as marbles!" Without waiting for anyone to answer, she turned to another group of people and started telling them all about the fabulous necklace her father had brought back from Europe.

Laughing, Nancy and her friends went back to filling their plates with food, but before they had managed to swallow more than a bite or two, Joanna was back. "I just can't stand it!" she said dramatically. "That gorgeous necklace is sitting in the house this very minute, and I just have to show it off or I'll die. I'm going to get it now, but you have to promise me that you'll never breathe a word of this to my parents. Okay?"

"Look, if your parents really don't want you to, maybe you should just forget it," Ned suggested.

"Right," George agreed. "Besides, I don't think anyone's all that interested in seeing it. Most people just want to keep on partying."

"Believe me, they'll forget about everything else once they set their eyes on this necklace," Joanna told them. "I'm just going to sneak it out, give everybody a quick peek, and then sneak it back. Don't go away. I'll only be a few minutes!" Giggling with excitement, she took off through the crowd, telling everyone what she was about to do.

Nancy laughed. "I don't know how she expects to keep her parents from knowing. She's already told everybody about that necklace."

"George was right, though," Bess remarked. "Joanna's the only one who really cares about it. I mean, an old necklace is nice, but I'd rather dance. Besides, at the rate she's moving, by the time she gets upstairs, the party will be over."

"Bess does have a point," Ned said as he watched Joanna make her way through the crowd. He turned to Nancy. "Come on, let's try to find a place to sit. I'm starving."

Carrying two plates of food, Ned started moving through the crowded living room, looking for a chair, a footstool, or even a clear space on the floor. Nancy followed, carrying two glasses of soda.

"I guess we'd better go out to the terrace," Ned called over his shoulder. "I don't see an empty square inch in here."

"Fine," Nancy called back. "I could use the air, anyway."

Together, they stepped through the sliding glass doors that led to the terrace. Just as they did, the band started playing again, and everyone began dancing. The couple closest to the doors whirled around and crashed into Nancy. One of the sodas flew up, splashing her face and hair, and the other fell down, soaking her blue skirt and dripping through her sandal.

"Sorry about that!" the couple called out, dancing away.

Nancy wiped her face with her hand, which immediately became sticky, too. "I was a little hot," she said, joking. "But I wasn't quite ready to take a shower." Glancing down at her skirt, she shook her head. "Well, it doesn't show too much, I guess."

"Sure," Ned said. "That big splotch looks like part of the pattern."

"Thanks a lot," Nancy replied with a laugh. "Yuck! Even my sandal's sticking to my foot. I've got to go wash it off. Be right back."

Pushing her wet hair off her forehead, Nancy threaded her way back through the crowded room, past the food table, and into a hallway. She had never been in the Tates' house before, but she knew a house that size would have plenty of bathrooms. She was right. She found one along the hall and another around a corner. Unfortunately, both of them were occupied.

Nancy kept walking down the hall, then took a right turn, and finally a left. She ended up at the bottom of a short stairway. Nancy climbed the few stairs and found herself in another hallway. She was in a different wing of the house then, she realized. It was quiet; the music from the band and the laughter of the guests sounded far away.

The hall was wide, with a deep, soft carpet and several closed doors on either side. One of them has to be a bathroom, Nancy thought.

Stopping in front of the first door, she raised her hand and was just about to knock when she heard something that made her hand freeze in midair.

It was a scream—a sharp, piercing scream—and it was coming from behind that door.

Chapter

Two

FORGETTING ABOUT KNOCKING, Nancy threw open the door and ran into the room. It was a study, with bookcases on three of the walls and a stone fireplace on the fourth. Next to the fireplace was a painting, which had been swung out from the wall like a cabinet door. Behind it was a wall safe, also open. In front of the safe stood Joanna. She was holding a box, staring at it in horror, as if she had found a snake inside.

"Joanna!" Nancy cried. "What is it? What's wrong?"

"Oh, Nancy!" Joanna's small face crumpled, and tears started rolling down her cheeks. "It's gone! I can't believe it! What am I going to do?"

Quickly crossing the room to Joanna's side, Nancy looked at the box she was holding. It was red leather, padded and lined with white satin. It had obviously contained a piece of jewelry—Nancy could see the imprint in the satin—and that piece of jewelry had obviously been a necklace.

"The diamond and ruby one?" she asked Joanna. "The one you just brought back from Europe?"

Sniffing, Joanna nodded. "The one my father paid a fortune for," she said miserably. "The one he's going to absolutely freak over when he finds out it's been stolen. What am I going to do?" she asked again. "If only I hadn't shot my mouth off about it!"

It was true, Nancy thought. Joanna had blabbed about the necklace to everyone, but it was too late to do anything about that. "What about the safe?" Nancy asked. "How many people at the party did you tell about the safe?"

"I didn't tell anyone about the safe," Joanna said positively. "I suppose somebody could have found it, but no one knows the combination except my parents and me."

"You're sure?" Nancy asked.

"Absolutely."

Stepping closer, Nancy looked carefully at the lock on the safe. It looked perfectly normal, so it couldn't have been broken into, or Joanna would have noticed. Whoever had taken the necklace knew how to pick a lock. Nancy didn't know every person at the party, but she knew most of them, and they were all perfectly regular River Heights teenagers. Not the types who knew about getting into top-quality safes or pulling off a big-time jewelry theft.

"When was the last time you saw the necklace?" she asked.

"Three days ago, when we got home," Joanna said. "I watched my daddy put it in the safe, and I haven't been near it since, until now." Her eyes widened. "You mean it could have been gone all this time and I didn't even know it?"

"Maybe," Nancy said. "Somebody could have gotten into the house, I guess, but I don't think they'd chance it while anyone was here."

"Then they wouldn't have had a problem," Joanna said. "I've hardly spent any time here since we got home, and the maids are both off till my parents get back."

"Listen, Joanna," Nancy said, "I know this

might ruin the party, but we have to call the police."

Joanna sniffed loudly. "I know," she agreed and burst into tears again.

There was a phone on the desk. Nancy crossed to it to dial the River Heights Police Department. After giving her name and the address of the house, she hung up and turned back to Joanna. "They'll be here in about fifteen minutes," she reported.

Wiping her eyes, Joanna grabbed Nancy's arm. "I just got an idea," she said excitedly. "I know the police have to be in on this, but, Nancy, you're a detective, too! And you're good, right?"

"Well, I've been successful before," Nancy said without false modesty. "What's your idea?" she asked, already guessing the answer.

"You try to find the necklace, too," Joanna told her. "I don't care if you work with the police or by yourself. Just help find that necklace before my parents get back. Please, Nancy, I'm really desperate! Will you help me?"

Nancy couldn't help but laugh. "I get it," she said. "If we find the necklace before they get back, then what they don't know won't hurt them, right?"

Joanna nodded.

"It sounds nice," Nancy said. "But with the police in on it, I really don't think there's any way to keep it from your parents."

"I guess not." Joanna looked ready to cry again, but after a few seconds, she cheered up. "But if the necklace is already back when they find out about it, it won't be so awful. I mean, how mad can they get if the necklace is safe and sound?"

Nancy laughed again. "I can't argue with that," she said. "Besides, I hate to say no to a new case."

"Oh, Nancy, thank you!" Joanna cried. "I feel better already. I'm just positive you'll solve the whole thing for me!"

"I'll do my best," Nancy promised. "But you've got to help me, too. You've got to tell the police and me everything you know. Don't keep something back just because you're embarrassed about it—like telling an entire party there was a valuable necklace in the house. And don't worry about the police," she went on. "I've worked with them before, and we get along fine. We'll all do everything we can."

Five minutes later, two men from the River Heights Police Department arrived, and Nancy met Detective John Ryan for the first time. He was about twenty-five or thirty years old, and he was handsome, with dark curly hair and blue eyes. He'd be even more handsome if he smiled, Nancy thought. Right now, he looks like he's at the end of a very bad day.

"I thought I knew just about everyone in the department," Nancy said after introducing herself. "You must be new."

"I've been working in Chicago," he said shortly. Looking past Nancy and Joanna, he nodded at the crowded party, which was still going strong. "Nobody's gone home, I hope. We'll have to question everyone."

"Oh, do you really have to?" Joanna asked. "These are all my friends. They wouldn't have stolen the necklace."

"You don't know that for sure," Detective Ryan told her. "Did you tell anyone here about it?"

Blushing, Joanna nodded. "Just about everyone," she admitted.

The detective looked grim. "You'd be surprised what some people will do for money, even so-called friends," he said.

"She didn't tell anyone about the safe, though," Nancy said, trying to be helpful. "All she said was that her father had brought back a necklace. I don't think anyone knew exactly where it was. Besides, whoever got into that safe had to have been a professional. I'm positive that no one that I know here could have done it."

Still not smiling, Detective Ryan gave

Nancy a long look. "Thanks for your opinion, Ms. Drew," he said finally. "Now, if it's all right with you, I'll get on with the official investigation." He told the other police officer to start questioning the party guests, then turned back to Joanna. "I'd like to see the safe now and get a good description of the necklace."

As the three of them walked to the study, Joanna leaned close to Nancy and whispered, "I thought you said you got along great with the police. So why is this guy treating you like you're contagious?"

"I'm not sure," Nancy whispered back. "He doesn't know me, so maybe he thinks I don't know what I'm talking about."

"Well, tell him who you are, then!" Joanna said. "Once he knows, he'll probably be glad to have you on his side."

Nancy turned and sneaked a look at Detective Ryan, who was a couple of steps behind the girls. He was frowning, and his handsome face looked as if it were carved out of stone. "I think I'll wait," she said. "I get the feeling he wouldn't be impressed even if I were Sherlock Holmes."

As Detective Ryan checked out the safe and talked to Joanna, Nancy kept her mouth shut, but she watched him closely and listened carefully. He knew what he was doing, that much was obvious. He asked all the right questions, and he even got Joanna to admit that she might have told a few people about the safe. Not anyone at the party, but maybe some people at the River Heights Country Club, where she had been spending her days.

"Joanna!" Nancy couldn't help butting in. "You didn't tell me about that. You said nobody knew about the safe."

"I guess I forgot." Joanna looked embarrassed. "But I promise, Nancy, that nobody —absolutely nobody—knows the combination." She looked at Detective Ryan. "I've also asked Nancy to help solve this case, and she said she would. She's a detective, too, you know."

As Nancy had predicted, Detective Ryan wasn't impressed. In fact, he looked disgusted. "A detective?" he asked, looking at Nancy.

Nancy nodded.

"An amateur detective, I take it?" Detective Ryan said.

Nancy nodded again. "But I've done pretty well for an amateur," she told him. "And as Joanna said, I promised her I'd help. So, please, let me know what I can do."

When he didn't answer, Nancy continued, saying, "It really doesn't look much like amateur work, does it, Detective? You did take a good look at that safe, didn't you? I think we're dealing with some pretty slick professionals."

Detective Ryan looked coolly at Nancy and raised one eyebrow. "We?" he asked. "What do you mean, 'we'?"

"I told you," Joanna said. "I asked Nancy to help solve this case."

The detective's eyebrow shot up even farther. "If you don't mind, Ms. Tate, I think I'll handle this one my own way. And that means using the police department, not an amateur detective."

"But I do mind!" Joanna protested. "Nancy promised she'd help, and I want her to."

"Sorry, Ms. Tate, but you don't really have any choice in the matter. I'm the detective in charge of the case, and what I say goes."

"Listen, Detective Ryan," Nancy said. "I don't want to butt in, but—"

"Good," he said, interrupting. "Then don't."

Nancy took a deep breath. Detective Ryan was beginning to bug her—a lot. "I was going to say that I guarantee I won't get in your way, if that's what you're worried about. I won't do any harm. And who knows? I just might help."

"What makes you so sure you won't do any harm?" he asked impatiently.

"I guess it's because I know what you have

to do to solve a case," Nancy explained. "I've solved some cases on my own, and—"

"That's fine, Ms. Drew," Detective Ryan said quickly. "You just keep on solving your own cases and stay away from mine." He started for the door and then stopped. Turning back, he pointed a finger at Nancy. "I warn you, Ms. Drew. Don't mess with this case."

Chapter

Three

LATE THE NEXT morning, as Nancy turned her blue Mustang into the entrance of the River Heights Country Club, she couldn't help but wonder. There she was, on the case, just twelve hours after Detective Ryan had warned her to stay off it. Should she continue or not?

Detective Ryan didn't know Nancy, of course, so he didn't know that telling her not to follow a case was like telling her not to breathe. But she didn't want to cross him, either. Still, she reasoned, she had promised Joanna she'd help, and she didn't want to let her down. If she was lucky, she could help without the detective even knowing about it, for a while, anyway. She just hoped she wouldn't run into him at the club that day. She wanted a chance to get started on her own before she had to deal with him.

Nancy was usually too busy to spend much time at the club. Despite her schedule, though, she seemed to have been there a lot recently. Before that, she had almost forgotten how peaceful it was, with its emerald-green golf course, its rambling stone clubhouse, and the tiled swimming and diving pools. That day, Nancy intended to follow Joanna and see whom she talked to at the club—and how much she told them about her possessions.

After parking her car in the lot near the clubhouse, Nancy took her green canvas carry-all and walked along the flagstone path that led to the swimming pool. The patio around the pool was crowded with people lounging, tanning, and sipping cool drinks. It seemed as if everyone was talking at once, but the first voice Nancy heard was Joanna's.

"I still can't believe it," Joanna was saying. "I mean, I had to beg my parents to let me stay at home alone, and then this happens! I just don't know what I'm going to do if that necklace doesn't turn up."

Joanna was talking to everyone in general, but the one who was listening the hardest was a tall, good-looking boy with sun-bleached hair and a peeling nose. He has to be a lifeguard, Nancy thought. She had never met a lifeguard who didn't have a peeling nose.

"Nancy!" Joanna called when she saw her. "I'm so glad you're here. I was afraid you might change your mind after the way that detective treated you."

Nancy smiled and shook her head. "Not a chance," she said, easing into one of the lounge chairs.

Sighing in relief, Joanna turned to the lifeguard. "This is Nancy Drew, Mike," she told him. "She's a fabulous detective, and she's going to find out who took my necklace."

"No kidding?" Mike gave Nancy a curious look. "What's your plan for finding it?"

Smiling, Nancy shook her head. "I don't have one yet," she said. Even if I did, she thought, I wouldn't talk about it.

Mike smiled back. He was still staring at her, and Nancy figured he must be a mystery buff. Either that, or he just liked the way she looked in her blue shorts and halter top. "It's kind of funny, though," he remarked, "that you're starting your investigation here at the club. This is nowhere near the scene of the crime, is it?"

"Oh, she just came here to talk to me,"

Joanna chimed in. "She doesn't really have any suspects yet."

"Well, I wish you luck," Mike said, getting ready to climb back up to his lifeguard chair. "Everybody here knew so much about that necklace that we feel like we've been robbed, too."

"Robbed?" a voice said. "Did somebody mention robbery?"

Turning to a woman who had just come out of the clubhouse, Joanna told her all about her missing necklace.

"I know exactly how you feel," the woman said sympathetically. "It was only two weeks ago that our Picasso disappeared. We had just come back from a trip, and we were going to have a party to show off the painting, but it disappeared." She shook her head and sighed. "Most people think we don't have a chance in a million of ever getting it back, either."

"What do the police say?" Nancy asked.

"Not much," the woman told her. "Detective Ryan thinks a professional ring of thieves is behind it and that our painting has changed hands at least five times by now."

So, Nancy thought, Ryan was on that case, too. It would be a nice feather in his cap if he could solve both of them by himself. No wonder he didn't want her help.

In a few minutes, the woman decided to go for a swim. Joanna wanted to get out of the sun for a while, so she and Nancy decided to go into the clubhouse lounge.

On the way, Nancy said to Joanna, "You know, I think it would be better if you didn't tell everyone I'm on the case. It just makes my investigation harder."

"Oh, I'm so sorry, Nancy," Joanna said, putting a hand on her arm. "I didn't think. I'll try to keep my mouth shut from now on. I promise."

"Thanks, Joanna," Nancy said as they entered the lounge. "That will really help."

The clubhouse lounge was a big, bright room with round tables and a long wooden bar on one side. As soon as the bartender saw Joanna, he smiled and waved her over. He was young, with dark curly hair, sparkling black eyes, and a friendly grin.

"That's Zachary," Joanna told Nancy, leading her toward the bar. "He's one of the nicest guys around." She introduced Nancy and ordered lemonade for both of them.

"How's it going, Jo?" Zachary asked, filling their glasses.

"Oh, Zach, it couldn't be worse!" Joanna moaned. "Remember that necklace I told you about?"

"The emerald one that some long-dead princess wore?" he asked.

"Diamonds, rubies, and a countess," Joanna said, correcting. "But it doesn't matter, anyway, because it's gone."

"What do you mean?"

"I mean gone, vanished, stolen!"

Zach gave a low whistle. "Uh-oh. I'll bet your father's really freaked."

"He doesn't know about it yet," Joanna said. "He and Mother are in Mexico."

Zach whistled again, shaking his head. "Boy, you people with money have problems I can't even dream about. You know Mr. Fairchild? Well, he was in here a couple of days ago, telling everybody about some rare book he had just bought. He was going away on a business trip, and he was really proud of the way he'd hidden the book."

"How was that?" Nancy asked.

"Right on the shelf with his ordinary books," Zach said. "He thought it was perfect —no one would think to look for a rare book there. Anyway," he said, going on, "I just hope Mr. Fairchild has a good security system, or he might find himself in the same pickle you are, Jo."

"Nobody could be in the same pickle," Joanna said. "They don't have to face *my* father." Then she brightened up a little. "But at least I have Nancy Drew working for me. She's a detective, Zach, and if anybody can figure out what happened to that necklace, she can."

Zach grinned at Nancy as he poured soda into a glass. "A detective, huh? That's great. I'm crazy about mystery books, read them all the time. What's your theory about the 'mystery of the missing necklace'?"

Before Nancy could answer, the telephone behind the bar buzzed, and Zach answered it. "Sorry," he said after he had hung up. "I have to get some drinks down to the men's locker room. Talk to you later, Jo." Grinning over his shoulder at Nancy, he said, "Good hunting, Detective."

After Zach left, Nancy looked at Joanna and sighed. "Joanna, you just promised me that you weren't going to tell anyone—"

"I know, I know," Joanna said, interrupting. "But Zach's my friend, and I didn't think it would matter if I told him."

"Joanna, it does matter—you could be talking to the thief!"

"Zach?" Joanna asked incredulously. "There's no way." As she took the final sip of her lemonade, she saw Nancy's exasperated expression. "Okay, okay. I won't tell anyone else."

"Please, Joanna. Try."

Joanna signed the check, and the girls headed back to the pool. As they strolled outside, they passed the tennis courts. "Oh, there's Max Fletcher!" Joanna said, waving to a young man who had just finished a game. "Everybody thinks he's the best-looking guy at the club. He's got the most money, that's for sure," she added. "He inherited his father's business—Fletcher Electronics."

Something about that name rang a bell in Nancy's head, but she didn't have time to think about it then. Returning Joanna's wave, Max Fletcher draped a towel around his neck and walked over to the two girls. He was tall and slender, with light brown hair and pale blue eyes. Joanna introduced Nancy to him and then told the story of her missing necklace again—without mentioning Nancy. Max, Nancy noticed, didn't seem too interested.

"Tough luck," he said, opening a new can of tennis balls. "Hey, can I interest either one of you in a game?"

"No thanks," Joanna answered for both of them. "We're a little busy now."

Max sighed. "Too bad. I could use some new competition to keep things exciting." Sighing again, he sauntered slowly back to the courts.

As the two girls continued on in the direction of the pool, Joanna realized that she had left her towel in the lounge. Since it was one of her own towels, they decided to return to the lounge to get it. As they walked, Nancy turned to Joanna. "Just how many people around here did you tell about the necklace, anyway?"

Joanna shrugged. "I don't really know," she admitted. "A lot, I guess. I mean, when you get something new, you just naturally want to tell people about it."

"But, Joanna, you're not talking about a new pair of designer jeans!" Nancy said seriously. That necklace is really expensive!" Of course, she thought, most of the people who belonged to the club also owned really expensive jewelry.

Glancing around the lounge, Nancy saw Mike the lifeguard passing by, probably on a break. He stopped to chat with two men, and Nancy heard him wish one of them a good trip. Zach came back and got into a conversation with a man at the other end of the bar about the man's latest big investment in the stock market. At a nearby table, three women were loudly discussing the trip one of them was about to make and the fact that her house would be closed up for a month.

"Well?" Joanna asked eagerly. "What do you think? Do you have any ideas yet about who did it?"

Nancy didn't answer. She had just realized

something. The lifeguard and the bartender had both known about Joanna's necklace, not to mention Max Fletcher and the dozens of others at the club who had heard her talking about it. People there didn't seem to think twice about telling everyone about the latest rare book or valuable painting they had just bought, where they kept it, and when they were leaving on a trip. Of course, Joanna hadn't been out of town when the necklace was stolen, but she had been at the club every day. And plenty of people knew that.

"I do have some ideas, Joanna," Nancy said finally. "But I can't talk about them yet. First, I've got to pay a visit to Detective Ryan."

"Sorry, Ms. Drew." Detective Ryan shook his head, not looking sorry at all. "I realize you want to help, but I told you before, this is my job. I'll do it."

"But doesn't it make sense?" Nancy asked. "Joanna's necklace and that woman's Picasso were both stolen, and they both spend a lot of time at the club. They—and everybody else there—talk all the time about what they've just bought and where they keep it. And," she said, leaning forward in her chair, "they don't bother to keep it a secret when they're going away and leaving their houses empty. If I were a robber, I'd jump at the chance."

Nancy had hardly been excited about seeing Detective Ryan again, but the more she had thought about the possible country club connection, the more sense it made to her. And even though Detective Ryan didn't want her help, she thought she ought to tell him her theory. As she had driven over to police headquarters, she kept her fingers crossed that he'd be interested. Instead, he was sitting with his blue eyes half-closed, as if he was about to fall asleep.

"Of course," Nancy said, "I still don't have any idea who the robber or robbers are. It could be just about anyone who spends a lot of time at the club—"

"Which really narrows it down, doesn't it?" Detective Ryan said, breaking in sarcastically.

"You know it doesn't," Nancy told him and then she smiled to soften what she had said. "What I'm trying to say is that I think it's worth checking out."

"Ms. Drew, I've got only so many officers," he said with a loud sigh. "Two for this case, to be exact. I've already had one of them out at the club, as a matter of fact, and he came up with zero. The other one's tied up on another case right now. But when somebody gets a free minute, I'll send them back out there. Will that make you happy?"

"I guess it'll have to," Nancy said. "I'm just

trying to help, that's all. I don't understand why you don't want me to."

"This is a matter for the police, that's why." Detective Ryan stood up, his eyes wide open now.

"I know that, Detective Ryan. Except that the police usually appreciate my efforts."

"They do. I've asked around about you. It seems you have a remarkable talent for solving crimes. But this is my case," he said in a tight, angry voice. "And last night, I told you to stay off it, Ms. Drew. I'm saying it again now. And it had better be the last time I have to tell you. Because if it isn't—"

At that moment, his phone rang, and Detective Ryan grabbed it. "What?" he bellowed. His expression changed from anger to surprise and back to anger. He scribbled something on a notepad, said, "I'm on my way," and slammed down the phone.

"Another robbery," he said to Nancy as he strode toward the door. "I suggest you go back to your amateur detecting and let me handle the real thing." Before Nancy had a chance to react to his latest insult, he was gone.

"Oh, what's the use?" she said to the empty office. "It would just make him madder if I told him about my cases, and I don't need that."

Then she noticed that he had left his

notepad behind, and she couldn't resist taking a look at it. When she did, she realized that Detective Ryan could warn her off the case until he was blue in the face, but it wouldn't do any good. On the pad he'd written the name Fairchild. Under that was an address, and under that were the words "rare book."

Victim number three in the country club robberies had just been nailed!

Chapter Four

"I STILL CAN'T believe you're actually going behind that detective's back, Nan," Bess said as she and George climbed into Nancy's car the next day. "I mean, I'm perfectly willing to help, especially since it means spending time at the club, but what if he finds out?"

"I don't know," Nancy said, pulling away from the curb. "Right now, I'm more interested in learning what's going on. I guess I'll just deal with Detective Ryan when and if I have to."

The day before, after she found out about Mr. Fairchild's stolen rare book, Nancy had done a little more snooping around in Detective Ryan's office. She'd discovered that there had been two other robberies besides the ones she knew about. And every one of the victims belonged to the River Heights Country Club.

A few minutes later, Nancy pulled her car into Ned's driveway. Ned gave Nancy a quick kiss after hopping into the front seat with her.

"Oh, Ned, would you mind taking your car? We might need two cars later."

"Okay with me. See you there," he said, pushing down on the door handle. Turning back and leaning into the open window, he asked, "Oh, by the way, what's my assignment, Detective?"

Nancy laughed. "We all have the same assignment," she said. "To listen. Listen for anyone asking questions about other people's vacations. Listen for anyone asking a lot of questions about anyone's new possessions. I don't know if it's a club employee or a member, but I'm convinced there's a connection between that place and the robberies."

"It makes sense to me," George said. "I don't understand why Detective Ryan's being so pigheaded about it."

"Actually, I think he knows there might be a connection, but he just doesn't have enough investigators to do anything about it," Nancy said. Then she laughed. "I guess we're giving him some extra support, whether he likes it or not."

As soon as the four of them arrived at the club, they split up, George heading for the tennis courts, Ned to the men's weight room, and Bess to the golf course. "I don't know a thing about golf, except that it looks extremely boring," Bess commented as she left. "I just hope the caddies are cute!"

After changing into her suit down in the women's locker room, Nancy decided to hang around the pool because she wanted to check out Mike. The day before, when she was there with Joanna, he had watched her carefully. Nancy had figured he was interested in her, but now she wasn't so sure. Maybe he was interested because he knew she was a detective and he was part of the crime. Of course, she was suspicious of just about everyone at this point, and Mike could turn out to be innocent, but she had to start somewhere. And on a warm day, the pool was the perfect place.

Sitting on a lounge chair, Nancy slipped off her sandals. She got up and walked to the edge of the pool. She was wearing a new yellow suit that showed off her long slender legs, and as she stretched her arms above her head, getting ready to dive, she could feel people's eyes on her. She just hoped one pair of those eyes belonged to Mike.

Nancy dived cleanly into the water, surfaced, then began to swim the length of the pool. She was tempted to stay in a long time since it was so cool and refreshing, but after three laps she decided to get out and start her investigation.

Most of the poolside loungers who had watched Nancy dive in didn't pay much attention to her as she climbed out and smoothed her streaming hair back from her face. But glancing casually around, she saw that Mike was watching her.

Good, she thought, pulling a comb through her hair. Let's see what he's really interested in. She sat on one of the chairs and started applying sunscreen. She had just started on her legs when she saw the lifeguard climb down from his chair and head her way.

"Hey," he said when he reached her chair. "Nancy, isn't it? You were here with Joanna Tate yesterday?"

"That's right."

"I thought so. Where's Joanna?" he asked. "She's here almost every day."

"Oh, she said she was too upset to go anywhere," Nancy told him. Actually, Nancy had asked Joanna to stay away from the club for a few days, so she could work without

Joanna asking her every ten seconds if she had found the necklace.

Hands on his hips, Mike gave her a big smile. "So? Solved Jo's crime yet?"

"I haven't even started," Nancy told him with a laugh. "If I'd solved it, you can be sure Joanna would have told the whole world by now."

"Yeah, that's true," he said. "Well, do you have any suspects?"

Nancy laughed again, hoping he wouldn't guess that he was one of them. "At this point, your guess is as good as mine. I really haven't spent much time on it."

"Well, I'm sure I don't know as much about solving crimes as you do." Mike grinned and started to go back to his chair. "But I'll bet you won't find your thief here in the swimming pool."

"You're probably right," Nancy said. "But I couldn't resist. Besides, exercise helps me think."

"Okay, I'll let you get to it," Mike told her. "Like I said, I wish you luck."

When he had finally gone, Nancy lay back on the lounge chair, trying to figure out if Mike was just being friendly or whether his friendliness was a cover for trying to learn how much she knew. Sighing, she realized it was much too early to tell about anyone yet.

Nancy stayed by the pool for half an hour more, listening to the conversations around her. Word of the stolen rare book had obviously reached the club, and everyone was talking about it. People were worried about their own houses, but Nancy noticed that the latest robbery didn't keep them from discussing where they hid their own valuable objects. She wanted to tell them all to keep their mouths shut. If Mike or anyone else at poolside was in on the robberies, then the rest of them were sitting ducks.

"Hi there," a voice said nearby. "It's Detective Drew, isn't it?"

Squinting into the sun, Nancy saw that Zach, the bartender, was standing over her, his dark eyes sparkling.

"I'm surprised to see you lying down on the job," he said, joking. "Joanna said you were a great detective, so I figured you'd be out trying to track down the necklace nabber, not soaking up the sun."

Sitting up, Nancy swung her legs over the side of the lounger and laughed. "Promise not to tell Joanna," she said. "If she finds out I've been swimming instead of looking for suspects, she'll never forgive me."

"My lips are sealed," Zach told her. "But just between you and me, do you think maybe the trail starts here at the club?" He shifted the tray of cold drinks he was carrying.

Slowly, without looking at him, Nancy slipped on her sandals. She needed those few seconds to think of what to say and how to say it. Suddenly she remembered what Zach had said about Mr. Fairchild's rare book. And at that moment it hit her—the trail did start there. She was sure of it! Maybe Zach was just asking an innocent question, or maybe he was in on the robberies. It didn't matter at the moment. What mattered was that Nancy suddenly realized that she had to be very careful. If the robbers were there, then they'd know about her interest in the case and would be watching every move she made.

"I'm not sure where the trail starts," she said, casually standing up. "But when I find out, you can bet I'll be on it. Right now, though, I think I'll go into the clubhouse and get something to drink. I've had enough sun for a while."

Smiling at Zach, Nancy made her way slowly into the clubhouse. Max Fletcher was there, she noticed, looking sleepy. When he saw her, he nodded and yawned at the same time, and Nancy wondered how anyone who was head of a big electronics company could be sitting around on a weekday. Then she realized that he probably had plenty of people working for him and didn't always have to go into the office himself.

Nancy ordered a soda, and Zach gave her a big wink as he served it.

What was the wink for? Nancy wondered. Sipping her soda she tried to relax. Forget him for now, she told herself. There are plenty of other people here to keep an eye on.

At that moment, one of those people came into the clubhouse. Mike the lifeguard, probably on a break, walked quickly inside. He looked around, frowned, and then moved off toward a stairway. Nancy took a last sip and decided to follow him. Going down the broad stairway, Nancy found herself in a long, narrow hallway and saw Mike just turning the corner at the end of it. Nancy walked a little faster, passing the women's locker room, and turned at the end of the hall. She passed the boiler room and saw Mike disappear into the men's locker room.

That lets you out, Nancy told herself. But maybe by some lucky coincidence Ned was in there, she thought. After all, that's why he had come—to check out the places she couldn't go.

Nancy doubled back down the hall, and as she passed the women's locker room, she thought that she might as well wash the chlorine out of her hair. She went into the bright yellow- and orange-tiled room, which had at least twenty shower stalls with glass doors.

As Nancy walked in, another girl, who was at the far end of the room, whirled around. She had short, curly carrot-red hair and big brown eyes. She looked frightened.

"Sorry," Nancy said. "Didn't mean to scare you."

"That's okay," the girl said quickly. "I was just leaving, anyway." Dropping a white canvas carryall on a bench, she hurried out of the room.

"Hey, you left your bag!" Nancy called after her. The girl didn't come back, but Nancy decided she probably would once she missed the bag.

Picking up her fluffy white towel, Nancy peeled off her bathing suit and stepped into one of the stalls.

The club is really serious about showers, she thought as she turned on the faucets. Not only was there the usual shower head at the top of the stall, but there was also a second one below it, aiming straight at her stomach, plus a third one on the opposite wall, which would hit her square in the back.

Might as well enjoy it, she told herself, turning the faucets up high. There was a strange clanging sound in the pipes, and in a few seconds the water, which was spraying full force out of all three spouts, turned scalding hot. Nancy reached out for the hot faucet and turned it all the way off, bracing herself for a blast of cold.

But the cold spray never came. The water stayed burning hot, and Nancy plastered herself against the shower door to get out of the direct aim of the spray.

Frantically, she pushed against the shower door, expecting it to pop open. When it didn't, her fright turned to terror. Her skin would start to blister any moment. Giving the door a desperate bang, she cried out, "Help! The door's stuck and I'm getting fried!"

Chapter Five

TRYING TO AVOID the water, she banged and shouted two more times until, finally, the door was wrenched open by a very surprised-looking woman wearing a large floppy hat and a flowered bathing suit.

Nancy scampered out and wrapped herself in her towel. "Thanks," she said. "I was beginning to turn from rare to medium."

The woman nodded. "It's a good thing I came back for my bag." She peered into the shower, which was still pouring out scalding water. "But I wonder what's happening. These showers were installed just a month ago," she said. As she talked, the woman went over to the canvas bag on the bench and picked it up. Looking inside, she frowned. "Funny. I was sure I put my watch in here."

"That's your bag?" Nancy asked.

"Yes. I have a bad habit of forgetting it," the woman said with a sigh. "And now it looks like I've forgotten my watch, too. I probably left it at home or up by the pool."

Nancy wasn't so sure about that. Remembering the redheaded girl who had dashed out of the locker room so fast, she had the feeling that this woman's watch was long gone. And if that was true, then she had better find out who that girl was. After all, if you're a thief, she thought, why stop with beach bags? Why not go for the big things?

"Oh, listen to me!" the woman said, slapping her forehead. "Here I am, worrying about my watch while you're standing there like a scalded cat! Come with me to the massage room. I'm sure Rita will have something to take the sting away."

Nancy had eased herself into the pair of orange shorts and matching top she'd worn to the club. She followed the woman down the hall. They were just about to go into the massage room when the woman spotted Zach coming around the corner and immediately called out to him. "You won't believe it,

Zach," she said angrily. "Those fancy new showers—one of them just broke and nearly burned this poor girl to a crisp!"

Zach looked at Nancy, worry in his dark eyes. "Are you okay?"

"Oh, sure, I'll be fine," Nancy said. "It felt like I was stuck in there forever, but it was really just a few seconds. The problem was, I couldn't get anything but hot water."

"And the door was jammed, too," the woman reported. "Zach, would you be an angel and call Maintenance to have that door fixed and then call a plumber? I'd do it, but I simply have to get home."

"Oh, that's right," Zach said. "Your daughter's coming for a visit, isn't she? Don't worry, Mrs. Ames, I'll call." He tapped the empty tray he was carrying. "I have to fill another order for the men's locker room, so I'll call from the bar phone." Smiling at both of them, he headed down the hall toward the stairs.

When Zach was out of earshot, Nancy commented to Mrs. Ames, "He seems to know everyone's business around here, doesn't he?"

"Oh, he's just a friendly fellow," was all Mrs. Ames said as she motioned Nancy into the women's massage room. "Now, let's take care of you."

The massage room was small, painted a pale yellow, and had soft music coming out of hidden speakers. On one of the two tables, a woman was stretched out on her stomach, having her shoulders and back kneaded by a small young woman with short blond hair, a friendly round face, and strong-looking hands.

"Rita," Mrs. Ames said, "I've got a casualty for you."

The masseuse turned away from the woman on the table. "What's up, Mrs. Ames?"

When Mrs. Ames explained what had happened to Nancy, Rita went to a white metal closet, pushed aside some jars and gauze, and brought out a small white tube of salve. "This should take care of everything," she said, handing the tube to Nancy. "But if it doesn't, I guess you'd better see a doctor."

"Thanks," Nancy said. "I'm sure it's not that bad."

"You never can tell," Mrs. Ames said with a frown. "Oh, I do hope Zach hasn't forgotten to call the plumber."

"Don't you worry, Mrs. Ames," Rita told her. "You know Zach. When he says he'll do something, it's as good as done."

"That's true," Mrs. Ames agreed, her frown disappearing. "Well, Rita, a massage would be absolutely divine, but I have to rush home and make sure the house is ready." Smiling at Nancy, she left the room and hurried down the hall.

Carefully, Nancy rubbed some salve onto her sore skin. "It feels better already," she reported, sighing as the stinging started to fade.

"Good. I thought it would do the trick." Turning back to the woman on the table, Rita shook her head. "Those new showers are really the pits. Sometimes I think they have minds of their own. I've been scalded twice since they were put in." She laughed. "But at least I was able to get out."

As if she'd suddenly woken up, the woman on the table raised her head an inch. "I've never had a problem," she reported. "And I use them every day."

"Then you've been lucky, Mrs. Davenport," Rita told her. "I can't keep track of all the people who've complained to me about them. Take my word for it," she said to Nancy with a grin, "those new locker rooms cost a pretty penny, but a penny's about all they're worth."

Nancy laughed. "I don't have to take your word for it," she said, smearing lotion onto herself.

"Just be careful next time," Rita advised as Nancy thanked her. "And come on back when your skin's okay. I'll give you a great massage."

Mrs. Davenport lifted her head again. "That I can agree with," she said. Nancy smiled and began to finish up. It was just about time to meet her friends.

Rita turned her attention back to Mrs. Davenport, who had already started to chat. "Now, Rita," she went on, letting her chin drop, "where was I? Oh, yes, that ancient Roman coin. You know, I always thought John's passion for coins was kind of silly. But I must admit, when he bought that one, even I got excited."

"Roman?" Rita asked, digging her strong fingers into Mrs. Davenport's shoulders. "I bet that cost a pretty penny, too."

"Well, I don't really like to talk money, but I will tell you this—it wasn't much under a quarter of a million."

Rita whistled, and Nancy wanted to do the same. Why was Mrs. Davenport telling Rita all this?

"My gosh, I didn't know one coin could be worth that much," Rita said. "If it were mine, I'd be afraid to have it in the house."

"I'm not crazy about the idea, either," Mrs. Davenport said. "But John insists. He says there's no point in having a collector's item if you can't enjoy it."

Nancy was ready to leave, but she waited, holding her breath, to see if Mrs. Davenport would reveal the hiding place of the expensive Roman coin. She wanted to shout at her to keep quiet, but fortunately the phone in the massage room rang, and Rita had to answer it. Nancy and Rita exchanged waves as Nancy left.

Moving slowly down the hall, Nancy realized that she had another suspect—Rita. People weren't any more closemouthed on the massage table than they were at the pool or in the bar, she thought. Of course, Rita could be totally innocent, just like Mike or Zach. She might have asked those questions about the coin just to make conversation.

But she could have another reason for wanting to know how much the coin cost—to see if it was worth stealing. And that remark about being afraid to have something that valuable in the house could have been a hint for Mrs. Davenport to tell her where it was kept.

And there was one more thing, Nancy realized as she climbed the stairs. Mrs. Ames and Mrs. Davenport were both surprised that the shower had broken down. But Rita swore that it happened all the time. Of course, all three of them could be right. But if the showers were fine, then Nancy had either been there the first time they broke down, or else the breakdown had been deliberate. If it was deliberate, she thought, then somebody is trying to scare me off.

Chapter Six

HALF AN HOUR later, sitting in a booth at Frank's Pizza with Bess and George, Nancy lifted a slice covered with green peppers and mushrooms and grinned. "This," she said, "is exactly what I need." She took a big bite, leaned back in the booth, and closed her eyes.

"Rough day at the country club?" George asked wryly.

"Don't ask," Nancy said, taking a sip of her soda. "First, tell me what you found out."

"Not much," Bess reported with a sigh. "If I ever have to lift another golf club, I just might hit somebody over the head with it. But the caddies almost made it worth my time," she said and laughed. "They're really cute, every one of them."

"Somehow, I don't think that's what Nancy's interested in," George commented.

"Sure I am," Nancy said jokingly. "Tell me more about the cute caddies, Bess. Did any of them have big ears?"

"I was getting to that," Bess said. "I couldn't tell if they were interested in everything the golfers told them, but they sure got an earful." She swallowed some diet soda and shook her head. "Almost all the golfers talked their heads off about very private stuff—including their possessions—and it was as if the caddies didn't even exist."

"But you said you couldn't tell if any of the caddies were interested?" Nancy asked.

"Not really," Bess said. "See, the people were talking to each other, not to the caddies."

Nancy nodded. "What about you, George? What happened on the courts?"

"A lot of great tennis," George answered with a grin. "The teacher—Jim Matthews—is a former professional, you know."

Nancy nodded. "He's good."

"He's fantastic!" George's brown eyes lit up

with enthusiasm. "There was this guy named Max Fletcher who bet Jim a hundred dollars that he could beat him, but Jim wiped up the court with him."

"I met Max yesterday," Nancy said. "According to Joanna, he wouldn't have any trouble paying up."

"That's for sure," George told her. "He took out a roll of money thicker than his fist and peeled off a hundred-dollar bill. Of course, Jim couldn't take the money. Anyway," she continued, "once Jim saw that I didn't really need lessons, we just played. He won, but I gave him a good game."

"Speaking of money," Bess remarked, "was he interested in anyone's? Max Fletcher's, maybe?"

"No way," George said. "After all, he didn't let Fletcher pay up on the bet. So I'd really be surprised if he were in on the robberies."

"Did anybody tell him about their newest fabulous possession while you were there?" Nancy asked.

"Sure, a couple did," George told her. "But Jim's the quiet type, and when anyone started talking about anything but tennis, he got even quieter, like he was bored."

"That could just be an act," Bess pointed out.

"It could be," George agreed. "But I don't

think it is. I think Jim loves tennis, not money."

"What does Jim look like?" Bess asked.

"Well, he's a little taller than I am," George said. "And he's got brown hair and the most beautiful brown eyes—" Suddenly she blushed. "Okay, I admit it. He's gorgeous."

"And you have a crush on him!" Bess announced. "No wonder you don't think he's up to anything. He could have picked your pocket and you wouldn't have noticed. You were too busy looking at his beautiful brown eyes!"

"Maybe," George admitted, still red in the face. "I still don't think he's in on it, Nancy, but I guess I'm a little prejudiced."

Nancy laughed. "It sounds like we all came up with zero today," she said, reaching for a second slice of pizza. "Wait till you hear what happened to me. I spent three hours at the pool and the clubhouse, and the only things I've got to show for it are a bunch of suspicions and a lot of sore skin."

"Too much sun?" Bess asked.

Nancy laughed again. "Too much water," she said.

Between bites of pizza, Nancy told them all about her hot shower and her encounters with Mike, Zach, Rita, and the redheaded girl.

"Really curly hair?" George asked. "And really red?"

"More orange. Like carrots," Nancy said with a nod.

"I saw her out by the courts," George told her. "And I heard somebody call her Cindy. She kept moving around, hanging out with different people, as though she couldn't make up her mind what to do."

"If you see her again, let me know," Nancy said. "Right now, she's my strongest suspect."

The three of them were still discussing the situation when Ned arrived.

"It's about time," Bess told him. "If you'd been much later, this pizza pan would have been completely empty."

Sliding into the booth beside Nancy, Ned laughed and reached for the next-to-the-last slice. "Sorry I'm late," he said. "But I gave the staff in the weight room a hand setting up a big new machine. Anyway," he said, "I've got news."

"What?" Bess asked hopefully. "Somebody confessed to the whole operation and we can all go home?"

"Not quite," Ned said. "But I think I've got a lead. I was in the locker room—which is a great place, by the way; they even bring drinks down if you phone for them—when a lifeguard came in."

"Mike?" Nancy asked.

"Right. That was his name. He took a shower, and then he was just hanging out, taking it easy, when this other guy came in and started talking to him about some vase he had just bought."

"A vase?"

Ned nodded, swallowing some pizza. "But not just any vase," he said. "It's from some ancient South American civilization or something, and it's worth thousands."

"And Mike was interested?" Nancy asked.

"A lot," Ned said. "I mean, I don't know if he's part of the robberies, but he asked all kinds of questions about it, including where the man kept it. And the man told him—right on the mantel over his fireplace. But that's not the best part." Ned paused to chew his pizza crust.

"Well, don't stop there!" Bess said, complaining. "Drop that crust and tell us what happened!"

"Sorry," Ned said with a laugh. "I'm starving. Anyway, the best part is that the man—Mr. Winslow—told this Mike that he's leaving on a business trip today and that his wife's going with him. He was leaving right then. They're probably driving to the airport now. They'll be gone for a week, he said, and while they're away the house will be empty. How's that for a robber's paradise?"

"It's perfect," Nancy said. "In fact, it's so perfect, I can't resist it."

"What do you mean?" Bess asked.

With a grin, Nancy turned to Ned. "Nickerson, how'd you like to be part of a stakeout?"

"With you?" Ned said. "Anytime, Nancy. Anytime."

At ten o'clock that night, Ned cut the engine on his car and let it coast slowly down the street, stopping it in front of the Winslow house. "The house isn't dark," he whispered, looking up the driveway at the three-story Tudor set back from the street and surrounded by tall trees.

"They probably have the lights on an automatic timer. Are you sure he said the house would be empty? No housekeeper or anyone?" Nancy asked.

"I'm positive," Ned told her. "Mr. Winslow said the housekeeper decided to take her vacation when she learned they were going away. And she's the only other person who lives there."

Nancy and Ned sat and watched the house for a few more minutes while Nancy decided on a plan of action. "Okay," she said softly to Ned. "We're going to have to split up. There's nothing or no one to prevent a burglar from entering at any of the other entrances. I'll find a nice little secluded place on the grounds where I can watch the back door. You stay here. If you see anyone approaching the house—anyone at all—hoot three times like an owl. Then follow them—but not too close."

"Is the hooting absolutely necessary?" Ned asked.

"Do you know how to make any other night sound to warn me? You can't yell, 'Hey, Nancy, intruder approaching on the starboard side.'"

"Okay. Guess you're right," Ned conceded, smiling. "You be careful, though, Detective Drew," he said, leaning over and giving her a quick kiss on the cheek.

Feeling a little like a thief herself, Nancy slipped out of the car and through a gap in the tall hedges that fronted the Winslow property. Once she was on the grounds, it was very dark. The stands of tall trees surrounding the house and grounds shut out some of the moonlight. Everything was in shadow.

As she drew closer to the house, Nancy became increasingly nervous, hoping she wouldn't trip a hidden electronic sensor that would set off an alarm. After each step, she waited, holding her breath and expecting to hear sirens start wailing. But when nothing happened after thirty or forty steps, she relaxed a little and walked more quickly.

Trying not to step on any twigs, Nancy moved cautiously around the house and walked as quietly as possible toward the back. About thirty feet from a back corner was a willow tree, its drooping branches swaying gently in the night air. It was a perfect place to wait, Nancy thought. The branches would hide her, but she could peer out and have a full view of the back and side of the house.

Once hidden by the low-hanging branches, Nancy relaxed a little and checked her watch. Ten-thirty. She just hoped the robbers would decide to show up that night. If they didn't, she and Ned would be up all night every night for the next week. Which would mean they'd have to rely on George and Bess to investigate the club during the day while they slept.

An hour later, Nancy realized that her left foot had fallen asleep. As quietly as possible, she stood up and shook her ankle, trying to get the circulation moving. The stinging, prickly sensation had just started to creep through her foot when she had to freeze, standing on one leg like a stork in sneakers.

A shadow was thrown up against the rear wall of the house. She could see the dark shape of a person slipping swiftly and silently toward the back door.

Chapter Seven

THIS IS IT! Nancy thought. The stakeout is paying off. The shadow was still there, sliding along the back wall. Her heart thudding, Nancy peered through the branches, hoping to catch a glimpse of the intruder.

As she watched, straining to see, the shadow suddenly began moving very erratically. It was looking for something—the entrance, maybe?

Wanting to see the thief, Nancy pushed a branch aside and poked her head out.

At the sound of the branches being disturbed, the shadow froze. For a few seconds, it remained motionless as though it were a piece of black paper pinned against the stucco and beams. Then, suddenly, it became smaller until it disappeared, and at the same time Nancy heard the sound of feet pounding across what must have been a stone patio. In a moment, the sound changed to a dull thudding as the person hit grass and kept on running.

Without hesitating, Nancy shoved the tangled willow branches apart and took off after her shadowy visitor.

Her foot still had very little feeling. Unable to control it, Nancy stumbled, scraping her knees and the palms of her hands on the rough stones of the patio. But she was up in a second, plunging into the darkness at the rear of the property. A feathery cloud had slid over the moon, making the night pitch-dark.

It was easy going at first, just a gentle sloping hill covered with thick mown grass. But after a couple of minutes, the grass ended, and Nancy found herself in a forest. Low-hanging branches caught at her hair and scratched her face, while dead wood and wet and slippery masses of leaves slowed her until she was almost taking baby steps.

When Nancy stopped to untangle her hair from a vine, she could hear the "shadow" ahead of her, crashing through the woods, not bothering now to be quiet. It wasn't moving quickly either, and Nancy thought she might have a chance to catch up with it. She was just about to plunge ahead, when she suddenly realized she couldn't hear the intruder anymore. Had he finally made his way through the forest? Or was he hiding somewhere ahead, lying in wait for her?

Deciding what to do in an instant, Nancy moved off again as quickly as possible, her arms stretched out in front of her. She expected someone to reach out and grab her at any second. But no one did, and after two or three minutes, she was abruptly stopped by a six-foot-high stone wall. So that's why the mysterious intruder had suddenly stopped making noise—the suspect had climbed the wall and slipped away, probably for good.

Nancy knew it was probably a lost cause by then, but she decided to continue. Maybe the person had fallen and she'd get lucky and find him lying on the ground. Besides, she had gone too far to quit then.

The trees hadn't thinned out, so Nancy easily climbed a maple tree and then stepped from it out onto the wall. The cloud drifted off the moon, and Nancy found herself looking out at a smooth lawn that stretched as far as she could see. Every once in a while, it dipped into a low valley or climbed a small hill, and there were a few clumps of trees here and there. It must be part of somebody's estate, she thought. But it's the biggest backyard I've ever seen.

Forget it, she told herself. The intruder could be anywhere out there. Your chances of finding him are about one in a million. She was just about ready to turn back when something caught her eye. Off to her right, something was moving. She was much too far away to tell what it was, but it didn't matter. If there was movement, Nancy wanted to find out who or what was making it.

Leaping lightly to the grass, she started running again, toward the spot where she had seen the stirring. After the dead leaves and branches of the forest floor, the grass felt like velvet underfoot. In only a couple of minutes, she found herself looking down a grassy slope at a small pond, and beyond that, far off, she could see lights.

Circling the pond, Nancy kept up her pace, all the time wondering whose property she was on. She focused her attention on the distant lights—which looked too bright to be from an individual house—so she didn't see the rock that suddenly tripped her. Falling, she threw out her arms, only to have her hands sink up to the wrists in sand.

A sandbox, Nancy thought, brushing herself off. But as she stood up, she realized that it wasn't a box. It was just a kidney-shaped bed of sand at the bottom of another small, grass-covered hill. And suddenly it hit her—she had fallen into a sandtrap. She wasn't standing in anyone's yard—she was on the golf course of the River Heights Country Club.

Like a shot, Nancy was off again, moving toward the lights, which she knew were the floodlights around the clubhouse. The shadow maker must have headed this way, too, she thought. And she wondered if he'd come from there in the first place. If he had, then that night's gamble had really paid off.

As Nancy drew closer to the clubhouse, she slowed down and strained her ears. Except for the gentle ripple of water in the pools, the complex seemed quiet. She edged her way to a set of sliding glass doors that led into the lounge and tested them.

They were locked. It was late—after midnight—there must not have been any dinner parties or meetings scheduled, and nobody was inside. But someone *is* here, Nancy thought.

Feeling certain that the mysterious shadow maker was close by, Nancy walked cautiously around the clubhouse, testing all the doors. Locked! But that didn't mean the intruder had gone. He might have a key. He could be in the clubhouse right then, watching and waiting to see what she'd do.

But what should she do? She hated to go back. But if she didn't show up at Ned's car soon, he'd come looking for her. And then he'd have the police out looking for her. And with her luck, it would be Detective Ryan.

Frustrated, Nancy turned from the clubhouse and started back, crossing the red tiles that surrounded the swimming area. That was when she saw them—several sets of footprints.

Her frustration disappearing, Nancy moved closer and bent down to examine them. A few pieces of grass and leaves were stuck to the tiles in the shape of footprints. They were facing the club, which meant the owner of them had probably came from the same direction she had.

Straightening up, Nancy followed the prints, which led her beside the swimming pool and over to the side of the square, twenty-foot-deep diving pool. It was dark there, the deep water was inky black, and the two-tiered diving platform looked like a visitor from a distant world.

Wishing she had a flashlight so she could see more clearly, Nancy took a couple of steps. Then she listened and stopped. Silly me, she thought. Just some leaves rustling.

Abruptly, there was a slapping sound on the tiles, and before Nancy could turn, she felt herself being shoved, hard, from behind. Her arms flailing wildly, Nancy fell, the cold, dark water of the diving pool meeting her with a slap.

Before she could orient herself, she felt herself being forced down into the watery darkness. One arm was viciously wrapped around her neck, and the other held her head just below the surface!

Chapter Eight

DESPERATELY, NANCY PULLED at the arm around her neck, finally sinking all ten fingernails into it. She would have given anything to know the identity of her partner in this lethal underwater ballet. But knowing wouldn't help her breathe. What she needed was air!

Squirming and thrashing, Nancy fought to free herself from the viselike arm around her neck, but nothing seemed to do any good. Suddenly, inspiration struck, and Nancy kicked, thrusting her legs deeper into the water. If she was going to drown, then her assailant would go down with her. Madly, she fluttered her legs, dragging them both toward the bottom.

The lack of oxygen was making her dizzy—her lungs were on fire, ready to burst. At what point her attacker had loosened his grip on her throat, she didn't know, but when the realization struck, she fought to pull herself through the water until her head broke the surface.

For a few seconds, Nancy bobbed in the middle of the pool, gulping in huge lungfuls of air. Then she forced herself to look around—her attacker had fled. She paddled over to the side, where she hung on and rested until her head started to clear and she got her breath back.

Then Nancy scanned the pool area more closely. It was definitely empty. Except for a second trail of footprints—bare, wet ones this time—everything looked exactly the same. Whoever had shoved her into the water was gone.

Nancy slowly dragged herself out of the pool. Sitting on the tiles, she pulled off her sneakers. She was too exhausted to pursue her attacker. Even if, by some miracle, she did catch up to him, she would only collapse at his feet.

Her head was pounding, and the last thing

she felt like doing was thinking. But she couldn't help wondering why her attacker had left the diving pool so suddenly.

Maybe, Nancy thought, he hadn't really wanted to drown her. Maybe he'd just wanted to scare her.

"Hey!"

Nancy jumped as a light blinded her eyes and an angry, harsh voice boomed out of the darkness.

"What are you doing here?" the voice demanded. "This is private property. Boy, I've had it up to here with you kids sneaking into the club, using the pool, trampling the golf course!"

And I've had it up to here with this whole night, Nancy thought tiredly. "Wait a minute," she said. "How do you know I'm not supposed to be here? I'm a member of this club, and so is my father."

"Yeah? Well, you ought to know the rules then," the voice said. "The rules say no one's allowed on the grounds after hours without a pass. Where's your pass?"

Good question, Nancy thought. "I forgot it," she said. "And you haven't told me who you are yet. What gives you the right to treat me like a criminal?"

Slowly, the light bobbed and came nearer.

As it did, Nancy was able to see who was behind it. A very short, very skinny man who didn't look like his powerful voice sounded.

"I'm the night watchman," the man informed her. "Your father—if he really does belong to the club—helps pay my salary. So I have the right to chase you off this property because it's my job."

Nancy suddenly sat up straighter. "When did you go on duty?" she asked.

"Ten, twenty minutes ago."

"Did you see anyone else?" Nancy asked. "Going in or out of the clubhouse, maybe?"

"Nope. I park at the front entrance, walk around the golf course, then cut over to the clubhouse. The place is locked up tight, just like it should be," he said. "I did think I saw someone jogging down the drive. Could have been one of the staff, but since he was on his way out, I didn't stop to check. Besides, I was clear over by the fifth hole."

"He?" Suddenly, Nancy didn't feel tired anymore. "What did he look like?"

"I told you, I decided not to check," the man repeated impatiently. "He was probably part of the staff, like I said. The staff can use this place anytime they want, and they don't need passes. You wouldn't believe how many kids like you decide to have midnight picnics and then leave their trash all over the grass."

"I told you I didn't—" Nancy stopped herself. Arguing wasn't going to do her any good, and if she told the truth, he'd probably call the police. "Look," she said. "You're right. Some friends of mine dared me to sneak in here and go for a swim."

The light swept around as the man observed her soaking clothes and drenched sneakers. "Shoes and all, huh?" he asked skeptically.

"Right," Nancy said, quickly. "After all, if I don't come back wet, they'll never believe I did it."

The night watchman shook his head, obviously disgusted with what he thought was a dumb prank. Then he surprised Nancy by giving a short laugh. "Maybe that guy I saw leaving wasn't staff after all," he said, laughing again. "Maybe it was one of your friends, checking up on you."

Some friend, Nancy thought. "Listen," she said, standing and picking up her shoes. "I've never done anything like this before, and, believe me, I don't plan on doing anything like it again. Why don't I just get out of here now, and we'll both forget the whole thing?"

"I'm not about to forget it," the man told her. "But I think your getting out of here sounds like the best idea you've had all night."

"You're right about that," Nancy said, and she started off toward the golf course.

"The entrance is that way," the man said, waving his flashlight in another direction.

"But I have to pretend I'm sneaking back out," Nancy called. "It's all part of the dare."

Shaking his head again, the man finally let her go. Nancy skirted the pool and the lounge chairs, moving quickly until she reached the golf course and was out of his sight.

So, she thought, as she headed barefoot toward the pond, the people who work here can come and go as they please. The night watchman must know them all, so if he sees any of them here at night, he wouldn't be the least bit suspicious. That's very nice. And if some of the people who work here just happen to be using it as a base of operations for a bunch of robberies, then that's also very nice —for them.

It could be someone on the staff, Nancy thought. But who? And what about Rita or Cindy? Just because it was a man who had attacked her in the pool didn't mean one of the women wasn't involved. She could be working with someone. Or a few people could all be working together.

How many people were involved, and who they were, Nancy didn't know yet. But she did know one thing—they were on to her. That night had definitely been a warning.

Well, Nancy thought, there's no way I'm

going to back off. I'm just going to have to be more careful, that's all. And she had to warn Bess and George and Ned, too.

Thinking of Ned, Nancy began to hurry. She'd been gone a long time—he must be going crazy, wondering what had happened. Once she reached the wall at the edge of the golf course, she forced her feet into the sopping sneakers, found a low point in the wall that had crumbled a bit, and climbed over.

The woods weren't any easier to get through on the way back, and by the time Nancy reached the edge of the Winslow property, she felt completely drained. A shower, she thought. A hot shower, then some dry clothes, and then food. A cheeseburger and a chocolate shake. And fries. Lots of fries.

Her stomach rumbling, Nancy passed the willow tree she had hidden beneath, hurried by the house and through the trees in the front, and finally stepped through the hedge and onto the street. Then she stopped, her mouth falling open in amazement.

Ned was still there. But instead of sitting in his car, he was leaning against it, his face turned sideways and pressed up against the roof as Detective John Ryan frisked him.

Chapter Nine

"HEY!" NANCY COULDN'T believe what she was seeing. "What's going on?" she shouted, running the last few yards to Ned's car.

Detective Ryan barely glanced at her. "What's going on is the apprehension of a suspicious character," he said. "Not that it's any of your business, Ms. Drew."

"Suspicious?" Nancy almost laughed. "Believe me, Detective, there's absolutely no reason to suspect Ned of anything."

"I suppose you know him?"

"Yes, I do. He's my boyfriend, Ned Nickerson."

"And I suppose you're going to tell me that he has a good reason for prowling around one of the wealthiest neighborhoods in town?" Detective Ryan continued searching Ned.

"I already told you the reason," Ned said, still leaning against the car. "I was looking for my date."

"That's right," Nancy said. "And here I am, so now you have to believe him."

The detective finally let go of Ned and turned to face Nancy. When he saw her wet hair and clothes, and the scratches on her face and hands, he frowned. "Is this the latest way to dress for a date?" he asked sarcastically.

"Of course not," Nancy said, trying to think of a way to explain things. "We were driving around, and—I thought I saw somebody sneaking around this house. So I got out of the car to look around, and Ned waited for me."

"Right," Ned said. "When she didn't come back, I went looking for her. I walked around the house, and then I drove around the neighborhood a few times. Then I decided to come back to the house one last time and look around. That's why whoever called you said I was prowling."

"Called?" Nancy asked. "You got a call about Ned?"

The detective nodded. "An anonymous tip.

Somebody reported a prowler on the grounds of the Winslow house."

"When was this?" Nancy wanted to know.

"Fifteen minutes ago."

Fifteen minutes, Nancy thought. Just enough time for my pool companion to get to a phone to call the police. He would have guessed I had to come back here.

"But I think I've answered enough questions," the detective said, breaking into her thoughts. "What about you, Ms. Drew? Do you always hop out of cars every time you see someone walking around a house?"

"No, I don't," Nancy said, knowing he wasn't going to like what she had to say. "But I knew the Winslows were leaving town, and I knew their house would be empty. They probably have a lot of valuable stuff in there, so I—"

"So you just decided to take things into your own hands," the detective said interrupting. "Look, Ms. Drew, I warned you before, and I'm going to warn you just one more time —stay off this case."

Without waiting for an answer, the detective opened the door of Ned's car and motioned Nancy to get inside. Ned slid in next to her and started the engine. Before he could pull away, though, Detective Ryan leaned down to the passenger window, a frosty look in his blue eyes. "Just one more thing, Ms. Drew. You never did explain why you're soaking wet. What did you do, fall into the Winslows' pool?"

"Well, it was awfully warm, Detective," Nancy answered. "And the water was very cool. Let's just say I couldn't resist it."

As Ned drove away, Nancy leaned back against the seat and closed her eyes. "I wanted to tell him everything that happened tonight, but I got the feeling he wouldn't have listened to a word I said."

"What *did* happen, anyway?" Ned asked.

"I did go for a swim," Nancy said. "But as I told Detective Ryan, I just couldn't resist."

While Ned drove through the quiet streets, Nancy told him what had happened after she left him.

"Joanna let the whole world know who I was, so that made me a very easy target," she said, finishing her story as Ned pulled up in front of the Drews' home. "But at least I'm sure I'm on the right trail. Whoever's behind those robberies has to have something to do with the country club. That's certain now."

"Right." Ned agreed and slipped an arm around her shoulders, pulling her close. "The question is who? And what are we going to do now?"

Nancy leaned back against him, relaxing for

the first time that night. "Keep looking," she said.

"But as you said, they're probably on to you. And that dunking tonight wasn't just for fun," Ned commented. "They're dangerous, and you've been warned to back off."

"I know," Nancy said. "I'll just have to keep my eyes open wide from now on. And so will Bess and George and you," she said, turning to kiss his cheek. "At least they haven't seen any of us together at the club. But we'll have to be careful to keep it that way."

After kissing him again, Nancy got out of the car and walked up to her house, her squishy sneakers leaving wet prints on the front walk. She remembered the prints she had seen earlier, and she knew she had to find out who had made them before he followed her again.

The next day, Nancy arrived at the club alone. Because George and Bess weren't members, Nancy had given them passes and told them to come individually, too. Ned was to stay away that day.

First, Nancy walked down to the tennis courts, hoping that maybe Cindy had decided to hang out there. She saw George and Jim playing a game, and she saw Max Fletcher. But there was no one around with flaming red hair, so she headed for the pool.

It was hot. The pool was packed, and Mike, as head lifeguard, was on duty as usual. He was too busy keeping an eye on the crowds to listen to conversations about people's valuables, or even to take a break. Nancy watched him for a few minutes, wondering if he was as good at drowning people as he was at saving them. He was big enough to have held her under water the night before.

Soon she went into the lounge, which was more crowded than the pool. Zach was working, as were two other bartender-waiters. They were scurrying around, filling glasses with soda, iced tea, and lemonade. Even Zach, who was usually so chatty, didn't stop at a single table for more than five seconds. He did find time to throw Nancy a quick wink; except for that, though, he was on the run.

Nancy had hoped to speak to everyone working in the lounge. If she was careful about the questions she asked, she might have learned something. But unless the crowds suddenly thinned out, she wouldn't get the chance.

There's still Rita, she thought. Even though it had been a man in the pool with her, that didn't mean Rita wasn't in on the robberies in some way. After all, she got an earful while she gave her massages.

When Nancy got downstairs, Rita was busy. Nancy wanted to wait and eavesdrop but decided that might be a little too obvious. Instead, she just asked if Rita had an opening, then walked down the hall to the women's locker room, where she locked up her bag. Might as well get some exercise while I'm waiting, she thought, and she went into the weight room.

Half an hour later, Rita stuck her head around the weight room door and told Nancy she could take her then. Her arms and thighs feeling like dead weight themselves, Nancy followed Rita into the massage room.

"Hop on the table," Rita said with a smile. "I'll loosen you up."

Within fifteen minutes, the soreness had left Nancy's muscles, and she felt so relaxed she wanted to take a nap. Rita knew her business, she thought.

"You look like you're falling asleep," Rita remarked, pounding Nancy's legs with the sides of her hands. "Want me to call up to the lounge and order you a drink?"

"I think they're too busy up there," Nancy said. "The place is jumping."

"Oh, right," Rita said. "Well, I've got a quick call to make, if you don't mind. It'll just take a second." While Nancy waited, her eyes closed, Rita spoke into the phone. "Just wanted to let you know that I can't make it," she said. "But I'll be in touch, okay? 'Bye."

Turning back to Nancy, Rita sighed. "Boy, am I glad to be inside on a day like this! I don't see how anybody can stay out in the sun when it's so hot. Of course, it's mostly the kids who do. The older people all come inside and sit around talking."

"Everybody's very friendly at the club," Nancy said.

"That's for sure." Rita laughed. "I can't believe some of the things people tell me. They talk about their love lives and their problems, their jobs—"

"And their money." Nancy finished for her. "The older people around here talk a lot about that, don't they?"

Laughing, Rita dug her fingers into the back of Nancy's neck. "Well, most of them have plenty of it, so I guess it's normal to talk about it."

"I suppose," Nancy said. "But I think if I were really rich I'd be more discreet about it."

Rita laughed again. "I would, too. If I had what some of them have, you can bet I wouldn't tell a single living soul."

But does she have what they have? Nancy wondered. Or some of what they have, like an antique necklace and a painting by Picasso? And if she does, how am I going to find out? Rita talks, but she doesn't really say much.

Five minutes later, Nancy decided to give up on Rita, for the moment, anyway. Yawning, she walked to the locker room. Just before she turned in the door, she saw a short, slender girl with hair the color of carrots come out of the weight room. It was Cindy.

For a second, Cindy stood completely still, her large eyes wide and staring. Then, suddenly, she leaped forward, brushed past Nancy, and raced for the stairs, taking them two at a time.

Nancy raced after her, up the stairs and into the crowded lounge. She glanced around, certain she could spot that hair anyplace, but there was no sign of it. Cindy couldn't be that far ahead, she thought, and she made her way as quickly as possible through the crowd and out into the pool area.

The patio was packed. Nancy looked everywhere, but there was still no sign of Cindy. Skirting the pool area, she was just about to head for the tennis courts when she heard the squeal of a car's tires.

Turning, Nancy was just in time to see a small yellow convertible peel out of the parking lot and head down the entrance drive. She was too far away to spot the license number, but there was no question about who the driver was. Cindy's hair looked as if it were on fire.

Frustrated, Nancy watched the car disappear down the drive. Cindy was feeling very guilty, that was obvious. But about what? Rifling through Mrs. Ames's beach bag? Or stealing from people's houses? Or both?

Still thinking about it, Nancy went back into the clubhouse and down to the locker room.

After she opened her locker, Nancy pulled out her canvas bag and was going to sling it over her shoulder. But then she noticed a white envelope sticking halfway out of the side pocket. Curious, she took it out and opened it. Inside was a piece of paper with a typed message. The message read: "We know what you're up to. But does your father? Forget about finding us, or we'll arrange a meeting with him—by the diving pool. How long can he hold his breath?"

Chapter Ten

"I UNDERSTAND WHY you're worried, Nancy," Carson Drew said after she had called him at his law office and explained what had happened. "But I'm leaving for New York tonight, remember? I'm going straight from the office. Actually, I have to leave in ten minutes or I'll miss the plane." He laughed lightly. "I think I'll be safe between here and the airport."

"I'm not worried about right now, Dad," Nancy said. She knew her father was leaving town—he was going to visit some friends and attend a lawyers' meeting in New York for a day or two. So she had rushed straight home from the club to warn him before he went. "I'm worried about when you come back. After all, you'll be home soon, and these people are serious."

"It certainly sounds like it," her father said. "Which is why I'm more worried about you than about me. Don't you think you should go to the police on this one?"

"I want to give it a little more time," Nancy said with a sigh. "I told you about Detective Ryan, remember?"

"I take it you two still haven't hit it off."

"No. He thinks I'm a giant pain in the neck." Nancy shook her head. "Anyway, I'm being careful. Don't worry."

"Well, I'm sure you think you know what you're doing, but just remember, you don't have eyes in the back of your head," her father said, warning her. "Forget about me, and look out for yourself."

Nancy agreed, but she knew she wouldn't be able to stop worrying. To have her father threatened was frightening. She was glad he was going to be out of town, but she couldn't stop thinking about what might happen when he came back.

As Nancy was pacing restlessly around the kitchen, going over everything she had discovered so far and not coming up with anything new, Hannah Gruen, the Drews' housekeeper, came in.

"You look like a cat stalking a bird," Hannah remarked.

Nancy laughed. Hannah had been with the Drews for fifteen years, and she knew Nancy's moods better than anyone. "I *am* stalking a bird," Nancy said. "More than one, I think. The problem is, I can't decide which one to go after."

"It's this new case, isn't it?" Hannah asked.

Nancy nodded, deciding not to mention the threat to her father. There was no sense in having Hannah lose sleep over it, too. Not yet, anyway. "I'm on the right track," she said. "But I don't have any concrete theories or clues. It's beginning to get pretty frustrating."

"Well, do you think wearing a path in the kitchen floor will help?" Hannah asked. Nancy glanced down sheepishly. "Why don't you play some music or do something to relax?"

"I guess I'll have to," Nancy said. Then she realized that she was still wearing the same sweaty shorts and shirt she had worked out in, and her hair was tangled and matted. "But first, I think I'll shower and change. It might not help me solve the case, but at least I'll feel human again."

"By the way," Hannah said as Nancy started to leave, "I'm going to a meeting at the library in a little while, so I won't be here for dinner. And since your father won't be here, either, it's leftovers for you."

"Fine," Nancy said, knowing she wouldn't be hungry, anyway. "I'll see you when you get back."

After a shower, Nancy dried her hair, put on a flowered cotton skirt and a white tank top, and pushed a rock tape into her tape deck. Bess and George might be home by then, she decided, and she wanted to find out if they had learned anything.

"Absolutely nothing," Bess reported when Nancy called. "It was exactly the same as yesterday, except there weren't as many golfers because it was so hot. The only difference was that one of the caddies was even more friendly to me than he had been yesterday." Bess giggled. "I was pretty friendly to him, too, which wasn't hard because he is *so* gorgeous!"

"Did you find out where any of them were last night?"

"Three of them talked about nothing but last night's baseball game, and they said they watched it at one of their houses," Bess said. "Of course, I suppose they could have been lying, but they discussed every hit and strike as though they'd been sitting in the stands."

"What about the other two?" Nancy asked.

"One said he was sick, and, believe me, he was croaking like a frog," Bess told her. "And Tom—he's the gorgeous one—well, he and I were talking on the phone for almost an hour. And that was at the time you were out getting soaked."

Nancy felt relieved. If Bess was right, then there were five people she didn't have to follow. "Okay, thanks," she said. "I'm going to call George now and see if she's got any leads."

"George has a date," Bess told her. "With her handsome tennis teacher. But she told me to tell you that he didn't act any differently today, either. She didn't find out what he was up to last night, but she's going to try to find out tonight."

"Good." For George's sake, Nancy hoped that the tennis instructor had a perfect alibi.

After she hung up, Nancy felt hungry and looked for something to eat. She found half a roast chicken and salad makings in the refrigerator, but it wasn't what she wanted. Remembering the cheeseburger and fries she hadn't eaten the night before, she called Ned and suggested they go out. Half an hour later, the two of them were sitting in a booth at the Burger Barn.

Nancy bit into a crisp fry and smiled. "If I

didn't have this case on my back, I'd be perfectly happy right now."

"Nothing new to report?" Ned asked.

"A little," Nancy said, telling him about her chase after Cindy. "I'd really like to talk to that girl. She's the only one I've seen who even acts suspiciously. She could have put the note in my locker. But that doesn't mean there aren't others in on it, too. Oh, Ned, I don't know. I really can't rule anyone out yet."

Ned smiled. "So what's your next step, Detective?"

"I guess I'm going to have to put their names into a hat, pick one, and follow that person after he or she leaves the club." Nancy laughed. "Maybe I'll get lucky."

"I don't think another stakeout would work, not at the Winslows' anyway," Ned said. "I have a feeling Detective Ryan has that covered. And I'm not so sure following these people is such a good idea."

"But I don't know what else to do," Nancy said, arguing. "I can't keep hanging out at the club—watching. They don't even do their dirty work there."

"They do part of it there," Ned reminded her. "They get all their information at the club. Plus, I just thought of something. The club would make a great place to hide stuff. It's got hundreds of lockers. And who knows? One of them might be filled with stolen goods instead of soggy towels."

"I didn't think of that." Nancy swallowed the last bite of her cheeseburger and grinned. "Did you ever consider becoming a detective?"

"Why bother?" Ned said with a laugh. "I've got you, remember?"

As Ned drove Nancy home, the two of them joked and laughed and talked about everything but the case. It felt good, Nancy thought, to forget about it for a little while. She decided to try not to think about it the whole night. Maybe all the clues would fall into place in the morning.

"Did I tell you how great you look tonight?" Ned asked as they got out of the car and walked to Nancy's house.

Nancy shook her head, smiling. "If you did, I didn't hear it. Go ahead, tell me again."

"You do look great," Ned said softly, reaching out and pulling her closer.

They were on the front porch then, and just as Ned was about to kiss her, Nancy pulled away, staring over his shoulder.

"What is it?" Ned asked.

"The door," Nancy said, pointing. "It's

partly open. And I remember locking it when I left."

"Maybe Hannah's home," Ned suggested, "and she just didn't shut it all the way."

Checking her watch, Nancy shook her head. "It's too early. And, anyway, if she were home, she'd have turned on the porch light."

Slowly, Nancy pushed the door open and stepped inside. She was sure Hannah wasn't there, but just in case, she called her name, three times. There was no answer.

Behind her, Ned said quietly, "I'll check the kitchen." Nancy heard his footsteps as he cautiously made his way into that room. She continued walking slowly through the house, peering into one room after the other. They were all empty, and nothing even looked disturbed.

Maybe I just didn't pull the front door closed tightly enough, she thought, trying to remember. It had never happened before, but there was always a first time.

Nancy was just starting to relax when she reached her father's room. One look, and her heart started pounding again. The door was closed. Carson Drew never shut it except when he was changing his clothes.

Her mouth dry, Nancy quietly put her hand on the doorknob, counted to three, and threw the door wide open.

A curtain billowed as the door opened, but nothing else moved. Slowly scanning the room, Nancy saw that the bed was made, the closet door was closed, the drawers were shut. Then her eyes moved up to the ceiling. There, dangling from the light fixture, was one of her father's neckties—made into a noose! Attached to it was a note scrawled in greasy bloodred lipstick:

> Your dad might be gone now, but he has to return sometime. We'll be waiting. Get off the case, Nancy Drew!

Chapter Eleven

STARING AT THE ugly message, Ned whistled softly. "Don't you think it's about time to call the police, Nancy?"

Nancy shook her head. "If it was anybody but Detective Ryan, I'd say yes. But he'd tell me it was all my own fault for messing around in police business."

"But if you tell him why it happened—because you're getting too close to the robbers—then he'd have to listen," Ned said.

"Maybe," she said. "But if he brings the police in and lets them swarm all over the country club, I guarantee there won't be another robbery in River Heights—at least not by these people. I haven't scared them off because they know I'm working alone and they think they can scare *me* off. But they wouldn't bother to threaten a whole police force. They'd just lie low until the whole thing blew over.

"Let's get this picked up before Hannah comes home," Nancy said. "If she sees this, she'll freak. I don't want her worrying about it until she has to. This just fries me," she said. "I know they're trying to scare me, and they have. But they're also making me very angry."

After Ned had left, Nancy forced herself to calm down so Hannah wouldn't notice that anything was wrong and ask questions. In her room, she turned on the TV, then snapped it off, put a tape in the deck, then immediately took it out. When Hannah came home, Nancy told her that she wanted some fresh air. She got in her car and went for a drive.

Nancy automatically turned toward the club. She didn't know what she was going to do there, but maybe she'd be able to get inside and explore—look in the lockers as Ned had suggested.

As Nancy was driving down the tree-lined entry drive toward the clubhouse, she thought of something that startled her. Her house hadn't been broken into. The door was just ajar, but it hadn't been jimmied, and neither had any of the windows. She was positive now that she *had* locked the door, so the only way anyone could have gotten in was with a key.

Nancy took her foot off the gas and let the car coast to a stop. She needed a minute to think it through. If the thief had used a key to get into her house, then maybe he had had keys for the other houses. But how?

Sitting in the car, Nancy went over her day—what she'd done and where she'd been. She had had her keys in her canvas bag, and the bag was with her the whole time.

Except, she remembered, when she had been in the weight room and when she had been having her massage. The bag had been in a locker then. Could someone have taken the key, made a copy, and put it back? Easy! After all, someone *had* put the note in her bag. Could it have been Cindy? Cindy certainly knew her way around the club.

Nancy thought of Rita, too. Could she have done it? Rita had never left the room. But Nancy remembered suddenly that she *had* made a short phone call.

What had she said? Something about being too busy to make it that night. Nancy thought she must have been canceling a date or something, and maybe she was. But maybe it was some kind of signal to let a partner know that Nancy's key was in a locker, there for the taking. Who could the partner be?

Nancy slowly backed her car up and out onto the main road. She drove about half a block until she came to a place where she could park so it would be half-hidden by trees. Then she walked through the grounds to the clubhouse. She decided it had been foolish to alert anyone that she was there by going up the driveway.

The clubhouse was dark and appeared to be locked up tight. But Nancy got lucky and found one open door. There were two choices: someone had forgotten to lock it, or someone was inside. Cautiously, she pushed the door open and stepped into the cool, dark silence.

Once inside, Nancy slipped off her sandals. She wished she weren't wearing a white top—it stood out like a neon light—but there was nothing she could do about it then. Taking a deep breath, she moved deeper into the building. Except for the occasional spill of moonlight slanting in from the windows, the club was night-dark. The silence was broken only by the faint ticking of a distant clock.

Bypassing the lounge, Nancy headed for the stairs that led to the locker rooms. She wanted to check out the locker she'd left her bag in to see how someone could have gotten in, left her that message, and taken her key.

There were a couple of yellow light bulbs burning downstairs, and they washed the hall in a sickly mustard glow. Walking soundlessly on the cool tiles, Nancy passed the locked women's massage room, the boiler room, and then turned into the locker room.

Using the weak glow from another yellow bulb, Nancy managed to find the locker she had used earlier. The key was in it, the same key she'd locked it with and kept in the pocket of her shorts. Most of the other lockers had keys in them, too.

That had to be it—the keys were interchangeable. Nancy took one out and tried it on another locker. No—it didn't work. Somebody must have used a key to get into the locker, though. Women went in and out of the room all day, and she couldn't imagine anyone taking the time to actually break into a locker. It was just too risky. Duplicate keys—

A faint sound. A bare foot on the tiles? Nancy froze and strained to hear it again. Holding her breath, she waited. She heard a car horn in the distance and the buzz of an airplane, and finally she distinguished the thudding of her heart. Then the noise came again, and Nancy whirled around—her hands were up, ready.

But the locker room remained empty. No one was looming in the doorway; no one was lurking in the shadows by the sinks.

Then Nancy almost laughed. The light was dim, but she saw it—a shining drop of water hanging from one of the faucets, ready to fall. When it did, she heard the gentle *plop* and realized she had been frightened by a slow drip from a faucet.

Her breathing returned to normal again. Nancy turned back to the lockers, thinking through her theory. The robber or robbers learn when a wealthy person will be away. Then they steal the person's house key from a locker room and have a duplicate made. But where do they copy the key? she wondered. They'd have to do it in the clubhouse; they wouldn't have time to take it away. And what about alarms at the houses? How could they break in without setting them off?

The faucet dripped again, an incredibly loud sound for such a small drop of water, and Nancy jumped again. Deciding she had had enough of the locker room, she stepped out into the still hallway. As she started toward the stairs, she noticed that the weight room door was open. As long as she was there, she decided, she might as well check it out, too.

Except for the spill of light from the hall bulbs, the weight room was all in shadow. The equipment, especially the big new weight-training machine, looked like monsters designed by a science-fiction writer.

Nancy walked into the middle of the room and realized that without a flashlight she wouldn't be able to detect much. Deciding to check out the room the next day, she turned to leave but paused by the new machine when she heard a noise that made her heart miss a beat. It wasn't water this time. It was a creaking sound with a faint jingling for accompaniment. The second sound was like the rattling of keys.

You've got keys on your mind, she told herself. As she took another step, the creaking-jingling sounded again. Nancy stopped and caught sight of the weight-training machine's shadow thrown high against the wall. The heavy piece of equipment was rocking slowly back and forth. But not by itself. Another shadow was next to it—the shadow of a person, both hands gripping the equipment, making the machine rock faster and faster. And as Nancy stood there, she realized that the machine was about to topple—straight onto her.

Chapter Twelve

THERE WAS NO time to wonder who was pushing the machine. There was almost no time to move. But Nancy did, leaping sideways, trying to throw herself out of the path of that lethal piece of equipment. She had no idea how much it weighed, but she did know that if it hit her, she could be killed.

With a thud, Nancy hit the hard floor, her shoulder and head skidding on the rough, scratchy carpet. At the same moment, the state-of-the-art workout equipment crashed. It bounced once, crashed again, and then rocked back and forth more and more slowly. Finally, with a creak and a clank, it stopped.

Slowly, Nancy opened her eyes and looked. Less than five inches lay between the tip of her nose and the top of the heavy equipment. If she hadn't seen the shadows on the wall, she'd have been pinned to the floor right then, beneath hundreds of pounds of bone-crushing equipment.

Nancy was just sitting up when she heard the door to the weight room slam and the echo of feet padding quickly down the hall. The contents of the room became obscure without the light from the hall. Knowing she couldn't possibly follow in time, Nancy closed her eyes and fell back on the dusty carpet.

No one could have known I was coming here tonight, she told herself. But somebody saw me, and the minute he did, I almost got caught.

Disgusted with herself for not being quieter and more careful, Nancy rolled quickly away from the workout equipment and started to get to her knees. That was when she noticed a narrow door in the wall next to her. Probably some kind of storage place, she thought. But then she remembered that the storage closet was on the opposite wall.

Nancy tested the metal handle. Locked, naturally. She knew she should get out of there and go home, but she couldn't stop wondering about what was behind that door. A set of duplicate keys for all the lockers, maybe? Or, better yet, a diamond and ruby necklace, a Picasso painting, a rare book, and all the other things that had been stolen?

After she opened the door to the hallway, she could see better. She rummaged in her large straw handbag for her lock-picking kit. She wished she could turn on a light, but she didn't dare risk it. Moving the small picks in the lock, she turned the tumblers by feel and sound.

A few minutes later, Nancy was staring at two packages of light bulbs, a small pile of rags, and, behind these, a void. Not much of a storage closet, she thought. She pushed the bulbs and rags aside and stepped in, stretching her hands out in front of her. She expected to be stopped by a back wall, but instead she continued to feel only air. She kept going, sure that she'd hit a wall any second—but nothing. She was in a long, narrow passageway.

As Nancy walked farther into the corridor, her hands felt nothing but the two walls on either side of her—no boxes, no spare equipment, nothing. It wouldn't be a very good storage room, anyway, she thought. It was so long and narrow that it would take hours to get anything from the back.

Nancy took a few more steps, then stumbled as her foot hit what felt like a loose tile. Instinctively, she threw her arms out to the sides to steady herself in the pitch darkness. But instead of hitting solid wall, her right hand pushed against a flimsy piece of metal that swung in silently and smoothly.

After Nancy regained her balance, she felt around with her hands, trying to figure out what kind of cabinet she had opened. She touched something soft and slightly damp. Pulling it out, she discovered that it was a terry-cloth towel. As she put her hand back into the cabinet—or whatever it was—she saw thin yellow lines of light spilling faintly into the cabinet. Her fingers reached out and closed around a plastic bottle; she removed it, opened it, and sniffed. It was suntan lotion.

A towel, a bottle of lotion, and yellow light. *This isn't just any cabinet,* Nancy thought excitedly. She was looking into the rear of a locker.

Wanting to make certain, she stepped back, ran her hands along the wall for a few inches, and then pushed again. Another metal panel swung in, and more lines of yellow light from the locker room fell into the locker. The same thing happened on the left wall.

It was perfect, Nancy thought with a smile. A perfectly beautiful setup. The door in the weight room, the little stash of light bulbs to make people think it was for storage, and the long line of locker backs, cleverly fixed so they could be opened and the robbers could help themselves to anyone's house keys. People in the locker rooms would not even be aware that one of the lockers was being rifled.

Nancy pushed open a few more locker backs. Even if she didn't know who was committing the burglaries, she at least knew how. And that meant she was one step closer to putting all the pieces together.

Nancy closed the metal panels and headed down the passageway and back into the weight room. As she passed the workout machine, lying still like some large wounded animal, she almost laughed. Whoever had pushed it at her had actually ended up helping her to crack the case! She was on to their secret now, and it was only a matter of time before she had them trapped!

Nancy gave the machine a pat, then gathered up her bag and the sandals she had dropped when she made her flying leap. She'd just left the weight room and was walking down the hall toward the stairs when a clattering noise made her spin around.

The noise went on for a few seconds. It sounded like rocks tumbling in a washing machine. Nancy saw that she was standing right next to the boiler room door. She pushed it open, and the noise got louder before settling down to a steady hum.

The pipes must be rattling, Nancy thought, or maybe the air conditioner had come on. Boiler rooms always had equipment that made loud noises. In the daytime, she wouldn't even have noticed it. And neither would anyone else, she thought suddenly.

On a hunch, Nancy stepped into the room and began looking around. In just five minutes, her hunch paid off. Stuck in a far corner, behind a pile of old pipes and covered with a dusty canvas sheet, was another piece of equipment. When Nancy pulled the sheet off, she found herself looking at a key-duplicating machine.

Perfect, she thought again. Anyone hearing the key duplicator would think it was just the furnace or the pipes and wouldn't check to see what the noise was.

Nancy had just left the boiler room when another sound made her freeze. Voices were coming from somewhere above her in the clubhouse. She couldn't tell exactly how many, but one was a man's, and at least one belonged to a woman. The robbers, she decided, coming back to check if the weight machine had done its work.

Quietly but quickly, Nancy padded barefoot the rest of the way down the hall, then ran lightly up the stairs. At the top of the stairs, she stopped, held her breath, and listened. The voices were coming from the lounge. She could hear them perfectly now, and what she heard made her burst out laughing. Fooled again, Detective, she told herself.

In the lounge sat Bess, George, and two boys Nancy didn't recognize. They were laughing, drinking soda, and obviously enjoying having the place to themselves. When Bess saw Nancy standing in the doorway, she jumped.

"Nan!" she said, surprised. "You scared me. What are you doing here?"

"I—I was looking for something. But now that I'm here, I think maybe I'll join the party," Nancy answered with a smile.

"Well, come on in!" the boy sitting next to Bess called out. He had brown hair and a very good build, and Nancy figured he must be Tom, the "gorgeous" caddy.

As Nancy took a chair at the round table,

George reached into a cooler and pulled out a can of soda. "Here," she said, sliding the soda to Nancy. "Jim and I brought these along, and they're still nice and cold."

Smiling at Jim, the tennis instructor, Nancy popped open the can and took a sip. "What is this? A late-night picnic?"

"Yeah," Tom said. "We ran into each other at Frank's Pizza, but it was so packed, it was sardine city. So we decided to come here to make our plans."

"Plans?"

"For tomorrow," Jim said. "It's the Fourth of July, and the club always has a big bash."

"We were just trying to decide how we're going to get together," Bess explained.

"When did you get here?" Nancy asked, suddenly changing the subject.

"Oh, about ten, fifteen minutes ago," Tom said.

"You didn't happen to see anyone leaving, did you?" Nancy asked. "Maybe somebody in a hurry?"

George shook her head. "The place was empty when we got here. I didn't even want to come in, but Jim said it was okay."

"The staff's allowed," Jim explained.

"So I've heard," Nancy said, wondering if it had been a member of the staff who had tried to bury her under a muscle-building machine.

It couldn't be Tom or Jim, at least she knew that for sure now, and she could scratch them off her list.

"Nan?" Bess broke into her thoughts. "What do you think? Should we all dress up in red, white, and blue for tomorrow?"

"It sounds kind of silly," George said.

"That's the idea," Tom said. "Everybody gets silly around here on the Fourth. But it's fun—you should see the fireworks display. It's amazing."

"Well, I'm going to wear a red, white, and blue hat, at least," Bess said, deciding out loud. Looking around the lounge, she laughed. "Hey, you know, this is the first time I've spent any time in here. I think I'll come more often."

"That's it!" Nancy said.

"What's it?"

"That's what you'll do." Turning to Bess, she grinned. "How'd you like to spend tomorrow here, in and around the clubhouse?" she asked. "You could swim and lounge around by the pool, you could have cold lemonade anytime you wanted, you could have a massage—"

"Sounds great!" Bess answered.

"There are only two things you have to do," Nancy said. "You have to have one short, easy little workout session in the weight room. And you have to talk. A lot."

"I think I can manage that," Bess said with a laugh. "Talking's one of my specialties."

The two guys looked completely confused, but Bess and George knew exactly what Nancy was up to. It was time for her to set a trap.

Chapter Thirteen

THE NEXT MORNING, Nancy shaded her eyes and looked up from her lounger beside the club pool. A sleek red Jaguar had just sped up the entry drive and swerved quickly into a parking spot near the clubhouse.

As Nancy and at least a dozen other people watched, Bess Marvin climbed out of the car, pulled out a designer-initialed duffel bag, adjusted her expensive-looking sunglasses, flipped back her shining blond hair, and sauntered slowly toward the pool.

Good, Nancy thought, smiling to herself.

Bess has everyone's attention. Now, let's see who's going to be the most interested in what she has to say.

"My gosh, it's crowded out here!" Bess exclaimed as she flopped into a chair not too close to Nancy's. "Is this the only patio?"

"Well, it is the Fourth. But we've been arguing for two years about expanding it," someone said. "Didn't you get the bulletins?"

"I just moved here," Bess explained. "We joined the club a week ago. I've been on the golf course, but this is the first chance I've had to use the pool. And would you believe it, the whole family's leaving town again tomorrow for a week."

"Well, on behalf of the staff, let me welcome you." Poor Mike was on duty again. He leaned down from his lifeguard chair and smiled, obviously attracted to Bess. "I hope you'll spend more time here once you get back."

Fingering what looked like a small teardrop diamond at the end of a silver chain around her neck, Bess smiled back. "Thanks," she said, and her hand reached up to touch one of her earrings. It flashed like a jewel in the sunlight, but like the necklace, it was a fake. A good one, but paste nonetheless. "That water looks absolutely wonderful," Bess went on, gazing at the pool. "If somebody will tell me where the safe is, I'll just get rid of my jewelry and go for a swim."

"Safe?" Mike laughed. "There isn't any safe."

Bess looked amazed, as if she'd never heard of such a thing. "But where do people put their jewelry when they want to go in the water?"

"Most people leave it at home," somebody else said.

"Oh, well, I leave the really valuable things at home," Bess said. "I mean, there are some things that never come out of our wall safe in the library. But this?" She held out the necklace and gave a little laugh. "This is just everyday stuff."

"Then don't worry about it," Mike told her. "Just put it in one of the lockers. It'll be there when you get back."

Looking skeptical, Bess stood up and walked into the lounge. Nancy waited a few minutes and then followed her, but just to the doorway. She wanted to keep a very low profile that day.

Ned, George, and two of Ned's friends —one of whom owned the red Jaguar—were sitting at a table, laughing and talking. Nancy had wanted Ned and George to be there to keep an eye on Bess.

Bess had stopped at the bar and ordered an

iced tea. Max Fletcher was sitting next to her, and Bess immediately struck up a conversation with him. Nancy grinned. Trust Bess to find time to talk to a handsome guy.

Finally, Bess turned to the woman next to her and spoke loudly enough for Nancy to hear. "What a beautiful emerald!" she exclaimed, peering closely at the ring on the woman's hand. "And what a beautiful setting. I've never seen one like it before."

The woman laughed, pleased at the compliment. "That's because there isn't another one like it. This is one of a kind. An old family heirloom."

"Oh, one of those. My mother has some of the most gorgeous pieces of jewelry, and they've been handed down, too. Someday they'll be mine." Bess sighed. "Unfortunately, they're all in the library safe, and that's where they'll stay until I'm twenty-one."

"Well, that won't be too long, will it?" the woman asked.

"No, but the thing is, we're going on vacation tomorrow," Bess told her. "We'll be spending an entire week with a bunch of people I've never met, and I'd love to make a fantastic impression. There's this strand of pearls with a diamond clasp that would really dazzle them."

The woman smiled, and Nancy tried not to laugh out loud. Bess was doing a perfect job. Practically the entire club now thought that she came from a wealthy family that had a safe full of valuable one-of-a-kind pieces of jewelry. And the most important thing was that they thought her house would be empty for a week. If nobody bites, Nancy thought, I might as well give up being a detective completely.

Bess turned back to Max Fletcher and started talking to him, not so loudly this time. Satisfied that things were going right, Nancy left. She had just passed the pool and was heading for the other side of the clubhouse when a girl with flaming red curls stepped out and hesitated in front of her. It was Cindy.

Nancy stopped, waiting to see what Cindy was up to.

Finally, after nervously clearing her throat, Cindy said, "I have to talk to you."

"I think that's a good idea," Nancy said.

"I want you to know that I put Mrs. Ames's watch back about an hour ago," Cindy said. "She's out by the pool. You can ask her. She's probably found it by now."

"It's nice that you put it back," Nancy said. "Is there anything else you have to return?"

Cindy looked confused and then angry as the implication of what Nancy said sunk in.

"What are you talking about?" she asked. "I never took anything else."

"Well, you took the watch. Why shouldn't I think you'd take other things?"

"Because I didn't, that's why!" Cindy cried. "Look, the watch is the only *thing* I've ever taken. All the other times it's just been money that people have left in their bags."

"All the other times?" Nancy asked.

Cindy nodded. "I know it's wrong, but I can't help it. It's like a game." She swallowed and pushed back her hair. "Anyway, when you saw me that time, I realized that the game was up. I put the watch back, and I promised myself I'd get help so I won't steal things anymore."

Nancy and Cindy stared at each other. Cindy seemed to be telling the truth, but how could she know for sure? Cindy dropped her eyes and backed away.

Just then, Ned and George came around the corner. "Nan," Ned said quietly. "Bess is just about to make her next move. You said you wanted to be there."

"I do." Still watching Cindy as she walked farther away, Nancy said to Ned, "I'll go into the clubhouse. You two stick with Cindy, okay? Don't let her out of your sight."

If Cindy's in on it, Nancy thought as she

headed back to the lounge, then she won't be able to warn anyone. And if she's the only thief, then we've got her.

The lounge was still extremely busy. It seemed as if every member of the club had turned out that day for the big Fourth of July party.

Extra waiters had been hired, and Nancy had trouble squeezing herself in at a busy table to order an iced tea from one of them. Zach was still behind the bar, she noticed, and Bess was just winding up her conversation with Max Fletcher.

"Well," Bess was saying, "since I do want to impress those people, I suppose I'd better get down to the weight room. I should have started working out a week ago—there's no way I'll lose five pounds in one session."

With a smile, Bess left the bar and sauntered slowly toward the stairway leading to the lower level. Nancy drank some of her tea, but she barely tasted it. This was the most important part of the trap. Bess was going to do a short workout, then have a massage. But before she went in with Rita, she was going to deposit her bag in a locker. If Nancy's plan worked, then somebody would use that little passageway to get to Bess's house key. If the thief was Cindy, then nothing would happen. But if the redhead *wasn't* the one, Nancy would catch the person right in the act.

At first, Nancy had planned to hide in the passageway or the boiler room. But that wouldn't be enough, she decided. She needed to catch someone actually going into Bess's house with the copy of the key they had made that day. She needed irrefutable proof.

Bess was gone by then. Nancy looked around to see if she could spot anything or anyone and that was when she saw Mike. He was standing in the doorway to the lounge, and he was looking toward the staircase.

This is it, Nancy thought excitedly. He's the one! He's going to follow her downstairs to see what she does. And when she puts her bag into a locker, he'll go into action.

Casually waving to a few people in the lounge, Mike strolled toward the stairway. Nancy waited until he had passed her table. Then she stood up and turned toward the stairs herself.

Zach was standing in front of her, his dark eyes twinkling as if he were really happy to see her.

"Hi, Nancy. Have you seen Joanna lately? She hasn't been around."

"Yes. I mean, no, I haven't seen her lately." Nancy looked past him, not wanting to lose sight of Mike, even though she knew where he was going. Then she smiled at Zach. "Sorry. I'm in kind of a hurry."

"Oh, no, I'm sorry. I almost forgot," he said. "You've got a phone call."

"Me?" Who'd be calling me here? Nancy wondered.

"That's right."

Mike had gone down the stairs then. "But there must be a mistake," she said. "Nobody knows I'm here."

"Somebody does," Zach told her and pulled on her elbow. "They asked for you. Come on. I said, 'Come on.' There's a phone at the bar. Take it there."

As he spoke, Zach had been propelling her gently but with authority ahead of him. She wondered about his behavior, but for just a minute. It was the worst possible time for a phone call. She'd miss Mike. Besides, she'd never be able to hear—the bar was three deep in people.

Just as she reached the bar, a sudden realization hit Nancy. Zach was purposely trying to keep her from following Mike. Could he be in on it, too? He has to be, Nancy thought. And he did practically shove me over here.

Nancy turned and faced Zach. He was still smiling, but his eyes weren't twinkling as they usually did. She forced herself to smile back.

She didn't want to let him know that she suspected him. It was much too soon.

Calmly, Nancy moved past the crowd and walked behind the bar to pick up the phone.

"Hello, Nancy," a female voice said. "I see you decided not to take our advice and get off the case."

Although she tried to disguise it, the voice belonged to Rita!

Chapter Fourteen

NANCY TOOK A slow, deep breath, hoping her voice wouldn't shake when she accused the person on the other end. "Hello, Rita," she said, surprisingly steadily.

"You couldn't stay away, could you?" Rita asked, dropping her disguise. "You just had to keep on trying to help your little friend, Joanna."

"Right," Nancy said. "Well, Rita, it's been nice talking to you, but I've really got to hang up now."

"Nice try," Rita said with a laugh. "But, Nancy dear, here's what's really going to happen. First, say goodbye to anyone you know at the bar in a real friendly way. We don't want anyone suspecting anything."

Nancy glanced over at the door leading to the pool, hoping to see Ned or George out there. No luck. She had told them to stay with Cindy, and that's exactly what they were doing.

"And then," Rita continued, "you'll do exactly what Zach tells you to do."

"What if I don't?" Nancy asked.

Rita laughed her usual friendly laugh. "Why don't you take a look at everybody's favorite bartender?" she suggested.

Nancy looked. Zach was standing right beside her. In one hand, he held a glass of soda. But in the other hand, hidden from everyone's view but Nancy's, was a gun, pointed straight at her. When he saw her notice the gun, Zach winked.

"Okay, I've seen it," Nancy told Rita. "What are you telling me? That if I don't do what he says, he'll shoot me? Right here in front of all these witnesses? That's pretty hard to believe."

"Well, you're welcome to put him to the test," Rita said. And she didn't laugh this time. "But I guarantee you'll be very disappointed."

For a second, Nancy was tempted to call

their bluff, if it was a bluff. But then she looked at the gun again and saw that its barrel was longer than usual. Looking more closely, she realized that it wasn't an extralong barrel; it was a normal barrel with a silencer on the end of it. The lounge was so crowded and noisy that a gunshot would sound about as loud as a pin dropping on the carpet.

"All right," Nancy said to Rita. "You win. For now, anyway. What do you want me to do?"

Rita chuckled. "As I said, do whatever Zach tells you. And no tricks, Nancy, or you'll be very sorry."

I'm sorry already, Nancy thought, hanging up the phone. Turning to Zach, she said, "Well? What's the plan?"

For an answer, Zach draped a dishtowel over his wrist, concealing the gun. Then he nodded toward the direction of the locker room stairs. "I'll be right behind you," he said, smiling so that everyone would think he was enjoying the company of a pretty girl. "Let's move, Nancy, okay?"

As slowly as she could, Nancy walked toward the stairs. But it wasn't slow enough. Ned and George didn't suddenly appear in the lounge to help her. No one even paid any attention as the two of them went down to the lower level.

As they walked along the hall, they passed the weight room, and out of the corner of her eye Nancy saw Bess. Her friend was on the rowing machine, going nowhere very slowly. It was easy to see that Bess was bored—she kept glancing around the room. Nancy was tempted to wave to get Bess's attention. Maybe Bess would see Zach, realize that something was wrong, and go for help. But just as she was about to raise her hand, Nancy felt something on her back. She was wearing a thin cotton top, and what she felt was cold and hard —Zach was pushing her ahead with the gun.

The hallway was empty. If Nancy was going to make a move, she knew she had to do it then. Pretending to stumble, she whirled around, aimed her left foot at Zach's gun hand, and kicked. The gun went flying, landing at the bottom of the stairs. Nancy started to race toward it and then stopped.

At the bottom of the stairs stood Max Fletcher. He bent down and calmly picked up the gun. He aimed it at Nancy. "Walk," he said softly. Nancy had no choice but to turn around and walk.

A few more feet, and they were at the door to the massage room. Max motioned with the gun, and Zach roughly pushed Nancy inside, then closed and locked the door behind them.

Rita was waiting. At the sight of Max, she

looked slightly surprised. Not as surprised as I am, Nancy thought.

"Don't be too hard on yourself, Nancy," Max said with a chuckle. "Except for ignoring me, you've been very clever. Of course, you wasted some valuable time with the lifeguard and that redheaded kleptomaniac." He chuckled again. "But there was no reason for you to suspect me. After all, I never did anything suspicious. And I'm a very wealthy man. Sole owner of Fletcher Electronics, a multimillion-dollar company that manufactures, among other things, the Fletcher Home Alarm System and wall safes. Maybe you've heard of them?"

Nancy stared at him. Now she knew why the name of his company had rung a bell when Joanna mentioned it. Fletcher alarms and safes were all over the place—in houses, office buildings, even cars. Home alarm systems, she thought. No wonder they were able to break into those houses without problems. Max Fletcher wouldn't have any trouble dismantling his own product. And if a house used a different system, well, that wouldn't stop him, either. He probably knew the competition's alarms as well as he knew his own.

"But why?" Nancy asked. "You have enough money."

"The challenge, Nancy," he said. "The excitement. Fletcher Electronics is boring.

Haven't you ever been so bored you'd do anything for excitement?"

Nancy didn't answer.

"Fortunately," Max said, "Rita and Zach shared my enthusiasm for a challenge, and I had no trouble getting them to join in my scheme. But, now that you know it all, I'm afraid we have to stop you."

Calmly, Max handed the gun to Zach. Then, with a nod and a smile to Nancy, he left the room.

She looked around quickly, hoping to spot a way out. Rita laughed. "Don't bother," she said. "There's only one way in and one way out, and Zach's covering it."

Nancy looked at Zach, who was leaning against the door, pointing the gun at her. Then she looked back at Rita. "Well," she said. "What now?"

"Let's get it over with, Rita," Zach said. "The sooner the better."

"Don't worry," Rita told him. "We have plenty of time." She smiled at Nancy. "I have to tell you, you really had us hopping for a while. We tried everything—the shower, the diving pool, the messages, the weight machine, but you wouldn't stop."

"Hey, Rita." Zach seemed very edgy. "I don't think Max wanted us to chat. Let's get this over with and get out of here."

Desperately, Nancy tried to stall for time. "I know you two could call each other on your phones to say when to get a key. But I hate to admit it, there's one thing I haven't figured out yet."

"I don't believe it," Rita said sarcastically. "The great girl detective doesn't have all the answers?"

"Not quite," Nancy said. "I don't know where you put the things you stole. So as long as you're going to seal my lips permanently, why don't you tell me? I'm dying of curiosity —excuse the pun."

Rita started to answer, but Zach broke in. "Okay, that's enough," he said to Rita. "Max left me in charge of this part of the operation, and I say we wrap it up and hit the road."

"Oh?" Nancy asked. "You're leaving town?"

"That's right," Rita said. "The River Heights Country Club has been very good to us, but you know what they say about too much of a good thing. Max says it's time to move on."

"Yeah, but there's just one thing we have to do before we leave," Zach said.

Rita nodded. "That's right," she said sadly, as if she really cared. "We're going to have to do something about you, Nancy."

"I don't suppose you'd believe me if I said I'd keep my mouth shut." Nancy could tell that Zach was getting edgier by the second, and she wanted to keep the conversation going. Anything to keep him from "wrapping it up."

"No, I wouldn't believe you for a minute," Rita told her. She was moving around the room now, closing cabinet doors and checking to make sure she hadn't left anything behind. "I'm surprised you'd even say anything as phony as that."

Nancy tried to laugh again. "Well, you can't blame me for trying. But since it didn't work, I think I ought to tell you that I do have friends here helping me. And if I don't meet them soon, they'll come looking for me. If they don't find me, they'll know something's wrong, and then you'll have the police breathing down your necks."

But Rita didn't seem threatened at all. "The police?" she said, raising her eyebrows skeptically. "The police were here once and went away empty-handed. Besides, we'll be long gone when they find you. And at that point, I'm afraid you won't be able to tell them a thing."

"Rita, will you just shut up!" Zach cried hoarsely. "If you keep running your mouth, somebody's going to turn up here."

Zach had obviously had enough, and Nancy knew that if she wanted to make a break for it, this was the time. She slowly took a step forward as if to follow Zach, then suddenly whirled around and started to swing the side of her hand down on Zach's arm.

But Zach was ready for her. Before Nancy could finish her move, he had dropped the gun and pinned her arms to her sides. Lifting her up, he tossed her onto the massage table and held her down, one hand over her mouth.

"My, my, Nancy, you're very tense," Rita said, clucking her tongue sympathetically. "You're lucky, though. I know all about relaxing tight muscles."

Nancy looked on helplessly as Rita moved to the table. Next she felt Rita's fingers tightening around her neck.

Nancy squirmed, twisting her body and shaking her head as hard as she could. She felt Zach's hand slip and immediately bit him on the thumb. He gasped and took his hand away. Nancy opened her mouth to scream.

"Don't do it!" Zach ordered, his dark eyes inches from hers. "One sound out of you and, believe me, I'll use this!"

Out of the corner of her eye, Nancy saw the gun—it was pointed straight at her temple. She closed her mouth.

"That's better," Rita said.

Again, Nancy felt Rita's fingers on her neck, then a sharp pain, and finally nothing.

Chapter Fifteen

SLOWLY, NANCY TURNED her head and opened her eyes. It was as black as when she had them closed. Her head ached, and she wanted to raise her hand to rub it. But she couldn't move her hands because they were tied behind her. Nancy then realized that her feet were tied also. She started to yell but discovered that her mouth had been taped.

One corner of the tape was loose, though, and by rubbing the edge against her shoulder, Nancy was able to peel it off. She shouted, but the only reply was the echo of her own voice.

Instinctively, Nancy began to struggle against the bindings that held her. All of her pulling and twisting only succeeding in scraping raw spots on her wrists and ankles.

Stop it, she told herself after a minute. Panicking won't get you anywhere. Breathe normally, and be thankful you're alive.

Nancy managed to calm herself and lay still on what felt like a hard floor. Her wrists and ankles were sore, and her head still ached, but otherwise she was fine. Which was weird, she thought, since the last thing she had seen before blacking out was the wrong end of a gun pointing at her head.

So Zach and Rita hadn't really meant to shoot her. Not right there in the massage room, anyway. Rita must have found some nerve in her neck that was guaranteed to send her straight to sleep. A pretty good trick, Nancy admitted. I'll have to learn that one myself someday.

But why hadn't Max wanted her killed yet? Nancy wondered. Well, of course, it was obvious. They could hardly haul a body through the crowded country club. They had stashed her someplace, and when they were good and ready, they'd come back and "wrap it up," as Zach had said.

That must mean I'm still at the club, Nancy thought. It would be too hard to get me out of here dead or unconscious. There are just too many people around.

But where in the club was she? Was she still downstairs, maybe in the massage room? It was possible. Rita could have closed up for the day and gone to join the holiday crowd.

Nancy tried to see anything that would give her a clue to where she was. The cabinets in the massage room were gleaming white metal, she remembered, and the tables were covered with white pads. Her eyes should have adjusted enough by then to see white, even with the lights off. But all she saw were black and dark shades of gray.

Cautiously, Nancy tested her wrists and ankles again. The ropes seemed to have loosened a little; she might be able to get free if she didn't rub her skin raw.

Moving slowly, Nancy sat up with her legs out in front of her. She decided to try to slip her arms under her legs and then shove her feet through the loop her arms made. That way, her arms would be in front of her, and she could untie her feet.

Digging at the knots with her fingernails, Nancy did eventually loosen them. When her legs were free, she discovered that they had gone to sleep, and she kicked them to get the circulation moving. Her foot struck something metallic.

She reached out with her feet again, and this time the metal gave a little. She scooted closer to the wall and shoved her foot against it as hard as she could. The cover moved as if it were on hinges.

As it flapped open, Nancy noticed thin lines of yellow light leaking in. When she realized what it was, she felt like smiling. She was looking through the back end of a locker. Zach and Rita had put her in the passageway between the locker rooms.

But suddenly, Nancy didn't feel like smiling. The time must be getting very close to when they would come back for her. The yellow light meant that it was night. The locker rooms and weight room were closed for the day. Nobody would be interested in using them, anyway; they were all outside, dancing and eating and waiting for the fireworks. No wonder no one had heard her when she yelled.

Max and Rita and Zach were probably up there, too, Nancy realized. And once the big bash was over and the club was deserted, they'd come for her. She didn't know exactly what they had in mind, but she had a feeling she'd be found the next day at the bottom of the swimming pool or out on the golf course, the victim of an accidental drowning or a bad fall. Of course, Ned and Bess and George would tell the police about her investigation.

But they wouldn't know whom she suspected. And by the time they figured it out, those two would be gone. And Max would be back at the tennis courts, making bets on games. He'd never be caught. He could even wait awhile, recruit more people to help him, and then start his whole operation all over again. I'm the only one who knows, Nancy thought. I'm the only one who can stop him.

Aware that she didn't have much time, Nancy bit down on the ropes holding her wrists and began pulling at the knots. The task was too difficult, and she felt like weeping. But then she remembered the light bulbs. She stood and walked down the passageway until she reached the end. It was the wrong end, though. Turning around, she worked her way back until she stumbled into the light bulbs stacked in front of the weight room door.

Breaking a bulb against the wall, Nancy put the base of it into her mouth and sawed at the rope on her wrists with the jagged, broken glass. Eventually, the rope frayed, and she pulled her hands free.

The door to the weight room was locked, naturally. But Nancy banged on it a few times, hoping that someone might hear her. No one came.

On her hands and knees again, Nancy felt around the floor, hoping to come across something she could use to pick the lock. She turned around and crawled in the other direction, sweeping her hands across the floor in front of her. By the time she reached the far end, she had picked up nothing but a lot of dust.

Nancy sat down and leaned back against the end wall, trying to decide what to do next. She heard something. Sitting up straighter, she listened closely. There it was again—the sound of cheering and clapping. Could the fireworks have started already? If they had, then time was really running out. She listened again. People were still laughing and cheering, but she didn't hear the pop or whine of firecrackers. They were probably just clapping for the music and laughing at their own jokes. Now, if she could just find a way to get out, she could join them.

Frustrated, Nancy banged at one of the locker backs with her fist. It swung in smoothly, just like all the others. Inside, she saw a pale blob of something. Pulling it out, she discovered it was a pair of much-used sweat socks. She started to stuff them back in and then realized how stupid she was being.

These are lockers, you idiot, she told herself. *Storage* lockers. Find something like a belt buckle or a barrette, and you just might be out of here.

Five minutes later, Nancy was a quarter of the way down the passage, rifling what must have been her fiftieth locker. So far, she had found a belt with the wrong kind of buckle, a deck of playing cards that were too flimsy to wedge open the lock, several combs and brushes, three dozen tennis balls, and enough dirty towels to start a laundry service. But she hadn't found anything that would help her get out.

Just keep going, Nancy told herself. There has to be something in one of these lockers that I can use. After all, people leave their keys in them; maybe they leave their credit cards, too. Or maybe a pocket knife or a nail clipper.

Pushing open yet another locker back, Nancy dragged out the usual wadded-up towel and then stretched her arm deep inside, hoping that this time she'd be lucky.

Suddenly, there was a screech of metal, and the thin lines of yellow light grew wide. Nancy's eyes had become so used to the dark by then that she squinted as if a floodlight had been turned on. Then she finally realized that the locker door had been yanked open—from inside the locker room. Before she had a chance to react, a hand had closed over her wrist, the fingers tightening in a powerful grip.

Chapter Sixteen

NANCY TRIED TO pull her arm back, but the hand only grasped tighter, the fingers digging into her arm and pushing it painfully against the sharp metal lip of the locker.

It would probably do her no good, but Nancy yelled, anyway.

"Hey!" a voice cried out. "Pipe down. This place is like an echo chamber, and you're breaking my ear drums!"

Ignoring the voice, Nancy started to yell again, and then a flashlight blinded her. Gasping, she put her free hand over her eyes.

"Well, well," the voice said. "You do get

yourself into the strangest predicaments, Ms. Drew."

Nancy gasped again, not because of the light but because she had suddenly recognized the voice. It was Detective John Ryan's.

Nancy let out her breath in relief. She wouldn't have to go poking through any more lockers, and she wouldn't be the victim of some "tragic accident" after all. She was safe.

After a moment, though, she realized that Ryan was still gripping her wrist and shining the flashlight in her eyes. She was relieved and happy that he was there, but she couldn't help feeling annoyed with him.

"Since you know who I am," she said, "why don't you stop trying to break my arm? And while you're at it, you might turn that flashlight off. I've been in this dungeon for hours, and my eyes have become very sensitive."

The detective immediately let go of her wrist and turned the flashlight away from her eyes. Nancy could see the knot of his dark red tie and the cleft in his strongly shaped chin, but his handsome face was in shadow. Then she heard a dry, throaty sound, and she realized that he was giving his imitation of a laugh.

"I'm glad you're enjoying yourself," she said wryly. "Do you want to share the joke, or is it private?"

"I'm afraid it's very private, Ms. Drew," he said. "In fact, I'm laughing at myself."

"Oh?" Nancy was surprised. Detective Ryan didn't seem as if he were the kind of man who could laugh at himself.

He didn't explain, though, and Nancy decided not to waste any time asking about it. "Never mind about the joke—whatever it is. How did you find me?"

"I got a call," he said.

"An anonymous call?"

Nancy saw his head shake.

"No, this one was very un-anonymous," the detective said. "Three people called me, and they all identified themselves. Bess Marvin, George Fayne, and Ned Nickerson. I assume you know them all?"

Nancy smiled. "Yes, I know them," she said. "They're my friends, and they called you because they knew I was in trouble."

"So they said," Detective Ryan commented. "Well, you can't say I didn't warn you."

Nancy could hardly believe it. She'd been threatened with a gun, tied up, and thrown in a dark, dusty passageway, and all he could say was "I told you so." She took a deep breath. "Aren't you interested in what I've found out?"

The detective's head moved up and down in

a quick nod. Nancy decided he was just too proud to admit that she might have solved his case and that his nod was the only hint she'd ever get that he really did want to know what had been going on. Quickly, but without leaving out any important details, she told him everything.

"Fletcher Electronics," Detective Ryan said when she'd finished, sounding completely disgusted. "It was right in front of my eyes."

"Mine, too," Nancy said. "Anyway, all I care about now is catching those creeps. How about getting me out of here so we can do it?"

The detective nodded, and after Nancy told him about the door in the weight room, he had it open in about three minutes.

"I think I know what solitary confinement means now," Nancy said as she stepped into the weight room. "Thanks for getting me out."

"Right. So give me a description," Detective Ryan demanded.

Nancy sighed. The detective obviously wasn't going to apologize for ignoring her for so long or thank her for helping to solve his case. Well, she told herself, I guess that's not as important as catching the thieves.

"I'm waiting," he said.

Quickly, Nancy described Zach and Rita and Max. "Listen, I know you've got a job to do. But we could finish it together. I think we ought to try to cooperate, at least until it's over. Deal?"

"Deal," he said after a couple of seconds. Together, the two of them raced for the stairs.

When they reached the lounge, they stopped and checked to see if Zach was at his usual place behind the bar. He wasn't.

"I guess that would have been too easy," the detective remarked. "Let's start checking the rest of the place." Without waiting for Nancy, he headed for the sliding doors that led to the pool.

At first, Nancy was so glad to be outside, breathing fresh air, that she couldn't decide what to do or where to begin looking for the culprits. For a moment, she just stood still, enjoying her freedom. When a hand touched her arm, she jumped and yelped.

"Steady," Ned said, putting his arm around her shoulders. "I'm one of the good guys."

"That's for sure," Nancy said, hugging him. "Thanks for calling the detective. I wasn't sure how much longer I'd have before Rita and Zach came back for me."

"So it *is* those two," Ned said with a frown. "When that lifeguard came back outside, I gave him the third degree, but he had about fifty witnesses to prove that he'd just gone to the locker room for some zinc oxide for his nose. George stayed with Cindy the whole time, and the girl didn't try to make a move. I figured it must be the bartender, but by that time it was too late."

"It doesn't matter now," Nancy said. "But it's three people, not two. The third one is Max Fletcher, and he's the brains behind the whole thing. Tell George and Bess, so they can look for him, too."

"Right," Ned said. "I'm going to check downstairs again, just to make sure they didn't slip back in there while we weren't looking. You might as well look around outside, but it's not going to be easy, Nan. It's almost time for the fireworks, and this place is a madhouse."

"Don't worry," Nancy said. "If they're here, we'll find them."

After Ned took off, Nancy looked around again. Now she knew what he meant by madhouse. The lounge, the deck around the pool, parts of the golf course, every place was filled with people waiting for the fireworks to begin. They weren't waiting quietly, either. Some were milling around with paper plates in their hands, some were dancing, some were swimming, and they were all talking and laughing at the top of their lungs.

The whole area was lit by torches, and

Nancy knew she'd have trouble picking out specific faces in the flickering light, but she stepped into the crowd, anyway. They have to be here, she told herself. They were planning to come back for her when the party was over, and they wouldn't want to go too far while they waited. Besides, Zach was the bartender. He had a job to do. And if he wasn't doing it in the lounge, then he must be outside, passing around trays of drinks.

As Nancy was edging her way through a knot of people, someone put a hot dog in her hand. She gratefully ate it while she continued searching. She saw Detective Ryan over by the swimming pool and caught his eye. Shaking his head, he gave her a thumbs-down signal.

Turning around, Nancy walked back to the lounge door, hoping that maybe Zach had returned for a refill. He hadn't, but on the far side of the room she saw Bess and George. When they spotted her, they waved and smiled, glad to see that she was okay. Nancy quickly joined them and explained who the thieves were. But neither girl had seen them, so Nancy decided to move on to the golf course.

Wishing she had another hot dog, Nancy pushed her way through clumps of people and finally made it to the smooth grass of the golf course. She stopped a second to take off her sandals, just in case she had to do any running. Carrying them in her hand, she started wandering through the happy crowd, checking every face but never finding the right ones.

Suddenly, the noise of the crowd seemed to get even louder. A cheer went up, and everyone started clapping. A man said, "This is the biggest one ever. I bet they'll see it as far away as Chicago." Looking to where he was pointing—at a small hill just a short distance from the crowd—Nancy could see where the fireworks display had been set up, and she realized it was about to begin.

Frustrated, Nancy turned around, and that was when she saw them. Two of them, anyway. Standing close together, Zach and Rita were looking at the hill, too. Zach raised his hand to point something out to Rita, and then he caught sight of Nancy.

Slowly, he lowered his hand, watching Nancy the whole time. Not taking her eyes off him, either, Nancy started moving in their direction. She ignored the jostling crowds around her.

Suddenly, when she was about ten feet from them, Nancy stopped walking. Zach hadn't taken a single step, and now she saw why. In his hand, barely hidden by a jacket tossed over his arm, was the gun. He raised it and pointed it straight at her. In a flash, Nancy realized that he was waiting for the fireworks to start before firing it. It was a perfect cover. Between the exploding firecrackers and the screams of the crowd, no one would hear a single silenced shot that would leave her lying on the ground.

Chapter Seventeen

As QUICKLY AS she could, Nancy glanced over her shoulder. The group of people in charge of the fireworks display had broken apart, and one man was checking his watch. Nancy realized that it was only a matter of seconds.

Looking back, she saw that Zach and Rita still hadn't moved. They were just waiting for the right moment.

Although there weren't crowds of people around her, there were people nearby. And Nancy knew that if she tried to protect herself, either she could lose Zach and Rita, or some innocent person could get hurt, or both. It wasn't worth the risk. She dropped her sandals and tossed her hair out of her eyes, but she stayed where she was.

The spectators became quieter. Shrieks of laughter died down to giggles, and loud conversations faded to soft murmurs. Nancy knew it was time for the fireworks—if she was going to do something, she had to do it then.

Before the first burst of a firecracker and the *whoosh* of a Roman candle shooting into the sky, Nancy ran and closed the gap between Zach and herself. And at the exact same moment that the club's most spectacular and biggest display got underway, Nancy leaped on him, both hands grabbing the arm that held the gun and forcing it straight up into the air.

The gun went off, its bullet shooting harmlessly into the sky, which was now filled with multicolored lights and bursting stars that glowed and then disappeared.

Nancy let go of Zach's arm with one hand, using it to dig her fingers into his throat. At the same time, she brought her knee up, giving him a sharp kick in the stomach.

Zach gasped and doubled over, and when he raised his head again, Nancy hit him on the jaw. Unconscious, he fell sideways onto the grass.

Breathing hard, Nancy looked for Rita, who was scrambling out of the area as fast as she could. Nancy stretched out her hand to grab the gun, when someone planted a foot on her wrist, pressing down hard and painfully.

Nancy looked up into the pale eyes of Max Fletcher.

"That was *very* exciting," Max said as he surreptitiously picked up and pocketed the gun. "But I'm afraid we've all had enough excitement for one night," he said to a couple of people who had glanced over to watch the antics on the ground.

Aiming the gun at her through his jacket pocket, Max said, "Come on, sweetie. Enough fooling around."

Slowly, Nancy got to her feet, keeping her eye on the gun.

"Oh, I'll use it all right," Max whispered into her ear. "Smile at anyone who looks at you, and walk nicely, or I will have to kill you."

Beside her, Nancy heard a low moan and realized that Zach was coming to. Rubbing his jaw, Zach got shakily to his feet and joined Max.

"Let's go now, shall we, sweetie?" Max said, smiling.

The fireworks were going strong; the sky was

lit up for miles, and the air reeked of gunpowder. Amazing, she thought, that just a couple of people even noticed what had happened. And they thought she and Zach were just goofing off.

As soon as they got close to the clubhouse, Nancy scanned the crowds for someone who knew her. If she could spot Detective Ryan, Ned, Bess, or George, she'd be all right. They'd *know* she was in trouble.

"Keep going," Max ordered, still in a whisper. "Around by the pool."

The crowd was thickest around the pool area, and Nancy hated the thought of getting into the middle of it. There wouldn't be room to try anything if she was packed in. But with a gun at her back, she didn't have much say in the matter.

As the three of them moved slowly through the crowd, a sudden shout went up. Nancy didn't pay much attention at first; it was probably just another reaction to the fireworks. Then she realized that the shout wasn't quite the same as the others she had been hearing. People weren't screaming in amazement over some fabulous pyrotechnic display. They were yelling because something completely unexpected had happened.

"I knew this was going to be a wild night,"

Nancy heard someone say. "But I still can't believe it. I mean, first the girl jumps into the diving pool with all her clothes on, and then the guy follows her, tie and all!"

A tie? Nancy thought. The only person who could possibly be wearing a tie to a Fourth of July party is Detective Ryan. And the only reason for him to be in the pool is that he's after Rita.

Glancing back, Nancy saw that Max and Zach hadn't paid any attention to the comment about the people in the pool. This was her chance.

Pretending that it was the only way to move through the crowd, Nancy began to make a path closer and closer to the diving pool. If I can get close enough, she thought, maybe Detective Ryan will see me.

When they reached the edge of the pool, Nancy looked down. In the middle of it, soaked to the skin, were Rita and Detective Ryan. Nancy was just about to call out when Zach spotted them. "Look," he said to Max. "It's Rita. She's been caught!"

"Too bad," Max commented. To Nancy, he whispered, "Keep moving. One word and I'll pull the trigger."

Nancy moved, but not the way Max had expected. She whirled around, reached out her arms, and shoved. Losing his balance, Max crashed backward into Zach, and, like two dominoes, they fell into the water.

In the water, Rita was swimming as quickly as she could toward the edge. But Nancy planted herself in front of her. "You can get out, Rita," she said. "But that's about as far as you'll go." Then she called to Detective Ryan, "Look out, Detective, one of them has a gun!"

"Not anymore!" he shouted back. Holding the gun out of the water, the detective motioned for Zach and Max to swim to the side.

Dripping wet, the three thieves climbed out of the pool, followed by Detective Ryan. By this time, George, Ned, and Bess had joined Nancy, and the four friends watched as the detective put handcuffs on the culprits.

As he started to lead them away, Detective Ryan turned back to Nancy. "Pretty nice work, Ms. Drew," he said. Then he left.

Bess gasped, amazement written across her delicate features. "Is he serious?" she said. "You just caught the crooks for him single-handedly. If it hadn't been for you, they'd be out of town by now. And that's all the thanks you get?"

"Forget it," Nancy told her. "The detective's just not the grateful type, I guess. Anyway, the important thing is it's over. Finally, we can relax a little and watch the rest of the fireworks!"

"It's just fantastic!" Joanna said, plopping herself into a lounge chair beside Nancy. "I mean, you caught them, you found my necklace, and my parents don't get back until tomorrow!"

It was the fifth of July, and Nancy was back at the country club. When she had called Joanna that morning to tell her that the case had been solved, Joanna had insisted on meeting her at the club. "I've been away too long," Joanna had said. "I need some sun. Besides, I can't wait to tell everybody what happened."

After the last few days, the club was the last place Nancy wanted to be, but she had finally agreed.

"I didn't really find out where they kept the stuff they stole," Nancy said now. "Detective Ryan made them admit that Rita had stashed it in her apartment."

"Oh, don't be so modest," Joanna said. "If it hadn't been for you, I'd be in big trouble. But now? As I said, my parents will be slightly mad, but once they know the necklace is back, they'll be calm about it all."

"Do you mind if I give you some advice?" Nancy asked.

"No, go ahead."

"Don't talk so much," Nancy suggested.

Joanna looked insulted.

"I mean, don't talk so much about the things you have," Nancy said quickly. "Especially the expensive things. And don't let the whole world know when your house will be empty. You never know who might be listening."

"Believe me, I'm going to keep my mouth shut from now on," Joanna said. Then, as she saw the lifeguard coming out of the clubhouse, she cried, "Mike! Guess what? Nancy found my necklace! It's a good thing I never told Max or Zach or Rita about that safe in the dining room, isn't it? That's where my parents keep cash, and I'm not talking about small bills, either!"

Shaking her head, Nancy decided to leave. Joanna would never change, but if she was lucky, maybe she'd never run into another Zach or Rita.

As Nancy walked toward her car, she almost bumped into Detective Ryan. He was wearing a striped tie, but otherwise he looked the same—grimly serious.

"Hi," Nancy said. "How did everything go after I left last night?"

"By the book," the detective said. "I just

came to tell Ms. Tate that her necklace will have to be used as evidence, so she won't get it back as soon as she thought."

"Uh-oh," Nancy said. "She's not going to be very happy about that."

Detective Ryan looked annoyed. "What does she expect?" he asked. "Does she think everything that happened was just a bad dream?"

"Something like that," Nancy said. "But don't worry. Even if she doesn't like it, she'll cooperate."

"Good." The detective started to walk away, and then he stopped. "By the way," he said, "I don't know if I told you, but you did a good job."

"You told me," Nancy said. "You said, 'pretty nice work.'" She laughed. "I expected you to say 'pretty nice work, for an *amateur.*'"

To her surprise, Detective Ryan shook his head, chuckling the way he had in the locker room the night before.

"What's so funny this time?" Nancy asked.

"Same thing," he said. "I might as well admit it. I was laughing at myself because I couldn't believe how stupid I'd been not to listen to you."

"I've got an idea," Nancy said with a grin.

"Why don't we try to work together from now on? We might solve more cases. And if it doesn't work out, well, we can always break the truce and start arguing again. Deal, Detective Ryan?"

He grinned back. "Deal, Detective Drew."

Nancy Drew
Mystery Stories

Nancy Drew is the best-known and most-loved girl detective ever. Join her and her best friends, George Fayne and Bess Marvin, in her many thrilling adventures available from HarperCollins

The Chalet School Series

Elinor M. Brent-Dyer

Elinor M. Brent-Dyer has written many books about life at the famous alpine school. Follow the thrilling adventures of Joey, Mary-Lou and all the other well-loved characters in these delightful stories, available only in Armada.

1	The School at the Chalet	£2.99
2	Jo of the Chalet School	£2.99
3	The Princess of the Chalet School	£2.99
4	Head Girl of the Chalet School	£2.99
5	Rivals of the Chalet School	£2.99
6	Eustacia Goes to the Chalet School	£2.99
7	The Chalet School and Jo	£2.99
8	The Chalet Girls in Camp	£2.99
9	Exploits of the Chalet Girls	£2.99
10	The Chalet School and the Lintons	£2.99
11	A Rebel at the Chalet School	£2.99
12	The New House at the Chalet School	£2.99
13	Jo Returns to the Chalet School	£2.99
15	A United Chalet School	£2.99
16	The Chalet School in Exile	£2.99
17	The Chalet School at War	£2.99
55	Jane and the Chalet School	£2.50
56	Redheads at the Chalet School	£2.99
58	Summer Term at the Chalet School	£3.50
60	Two Sams at the Chalet School	£2.99

Order Form

To order direct from the publishers, just make a list of the titles you want and fill in the form below:

Name ....

Address ....

....

....

Send to: Dept 6, HarperCollins Publishers Ltd, Westerhill Road, Bishopbriggs, Glasgow G64 2QT.

Please enclose a cheque or postal order to the value of the cover price, plus:

UK & BFPO: Add £1.00 for the first book, and 25p per copy for each addition book ordered.

Overseas and Eire: Add £2.95 service charge. Books will be sent by surface mail but quotes for airmail despatch will be given on request.

A 24-hour telephone ordering service is avail-able to Visa and Access card holders: 041-772 2281